KARMA

LAUREN BIEL

Library of Congress Cataloging-in-Publication Data

Karma/Lauren Biel 1st ed.

Cover Design: DesignbyCharlyy

Editing: Sugar Free Editing

Interior Design: Sugar Free Editing

For more information on this book and the author, visit: www.LaurenBiel.com

Please visit LaurenBiel.com for a full list of content warnings.

CHAPTER 1

KNOX

I double-check the list before I enter the building. Mr. Warrenthal. He deserted the Exodus three years ago, and they've been waiting for the Reckoning so that I can take him out.

The problem is, Mr. Warrenthal is very aware of the impending crime-free night and, to prepare, he has booked a ticket out of Vail. He's supposed to leave this morning. When the Elders got wind of it—they seem to have connections everywhere—they sent me to intercept him. I had no choice but to throw on clothes before the sun rose and head over to the mansion at the base of the mountain.

I put on gloves before I head inside. He shouldn't be expecting me, but he has to know this is coming. No one leaves the Exodus. You can't just decide you're bored with your rich, privileged life and quit the society that made you who you are.

I should know. They made me who I am now.

"Surprise," I say as I find him in bed. His packed suitcases stand beside the ornate footboard. The elders' intel was right.

With eyes so wide that I can see every bit of white, the man sits up in bed. "No, no, no!" he pleads. "The Bishop gave me grace to leave the society!"

"You and I both know that's not true."

"It is!"

"I wouldn't be here if it was."

"I have money!"

"Of course you do. You all do."

But I do not. Wallowing in vast riches wasn't part of the contract I entered into almost ten years ago. Having been *brought* to the Exodus instead of *born into* the Exodus, I was granted my life and nothing more.

The man's plea falls on deaf ears. The targets always offer huge sums of cash, but I don't waver from my mission. I have a job to do, and if I fail, my name will go on a list, and someone will visit me next. Someone just like me.

A hitman.

Their pawn.

The worker bee in their intricate hive.

Because I'm theirs.

I've sold my soul to the devil, and now I'm his watcher. His henchman. A pawn in a system I wasn't born into. I was taken and given a choice. I could be the executioner or the sacrifice. Since I'm not a farm animal who's destined to be bled and rendered for their use, I chose to join them.

But I didn't get to become one of them. Not really. I was allowed to keep my life, but the life I live no longer belongs to me.

Sometimes I wonder if it would have been better to have bled out in their glamorous cabin in the woods. At least the blood soaking their fancy hardwood floors would be my own. At least I would have died free.

A crowbar hangs by my side, and one quick smack of it against the side of the man's skull stops his annoying begging.

I fasten a thick rope around his limp wrists and ankles, then drag him out of bed. I don't like to kill them in bed, preferring to position them in their luxurious living rooms instead. It's so ironic to die in the room in which you should live.

I drop his heavy body onto a leather chair and hit a button to make it recline. At least he can be comfortable as he dies, reclining in a room littered with original artworks and first printings and the perfume of expensive cigars.

Three remotes lie on the table beside us, and I pick them up and play with them until stereo speakers drop from the ceiling. I sway and spin around the chair as I work a knife from my hip to the opening of "Bohemian Rhapsody" by Queen. I sing every word as I wait for him to wake up.

As if it had been scripted, his eyes pop open just as the song ascends into greatness, and my blade sinks into the side of his neck. In and out, the knife plunges in and pulls back with the beat. A remote gurgle precedes a spurt of blood from his neck, which fountains out in a ferocious spray of red. The walls drip with the stuff. I rip the metal from his skin a final time and put my fingers beneath his chin, lowering his lax jaw so that it looks as if he's singing the lyrics with his mouth. My bloody puppet.

The song climaxes, and then the endnote makes way for silence. Blood paints the walls of his gaudy mansion like some kind of abstract art installation. Too bad I can't slap a high-dollar price tag on it and sell it to the rich and bored.

The blood slows to a trickle and travels down his stained shirt. I pull the list from my pocket and dip my gloved finger into the crimson puddle beneath him. After spreading the paper on my thigh, I find his name and brush red across it.

One down. As many as they need to go.

I head outside and hear a meow in the bushes beside the door. I squat on the sidewalk and meow back like a lunatic. A little gray cat pokes its head from beneath the thick foliage. I hold my hand toward it, and it takes a perfunctory sniff before brushing a warm, furry cheek against my curled fingers. A pinprick of regret stabs my chest as I wonder if I've just killed this cat's only source of care.

"I hope I didn't just murder your dad," I say, giving it another pat. I didn't see any signs of a cat inside, though. No food. No toys lying around.

I fucking love animals and would take this guy with me if I didn't already have a menu item hopping around at home. Even though Petey would probably wipe the floor with the biggest cat, I can't chance it.

I stand and leave the little cat behind. I can't let it get to me. Cats are suburban apex predators, and that guy can certainly fend for himself. I also have no time to meander when today is such a big day for the society.

Tonight, the Exodus elders are hosting their ten-hour party in the very same mountains I was dragged to nearly a decade ago. Half the participants care about little more than fun and fucking, but the rest are there to participate in the old traditions.

Killing sacrificial lambs on their treasured night.

The Reckoning is a night to experience your most carnal desires, no matter how sinful they may be. Do you want to fuck your friend's wife? Kill her, maybe? Go nuts. Just so long as those you wish to harm weren't born into the group, that is.

The Exodus doesn't kill off members who were born into their ranks, but people like me are and will always be fair game. Just like the rest of the town. Anyone who isn't locked away or gone for the weekend can and will be killed by any of the men or women who choose hunting over staying behind and fucking.

That's the dividing line within the group.

At one point, I would have been content to stay back and fuck the beautiful women who are way above my class, but since Exodus has broken me down and reshaped me into the monster I am now, I go out and kill. I have to, even if I don't want to.

No one says no to the Exodus.

I certainly didn't.

I check the time on my cell phone. My next appointment isn't for thirty minutes, but at least I don't have to kill anyone. I just have to pick up my suit from the dry cleaner. The menial task shouldn't feel so pressing, but I need my suit for tonight, and the dry-cleaning staff are eager to get out of town. I take the winding back roads until I pull onto Main Street.

The dry cleaner is nestled among a few other shops. There's even a grocery store in the middle—the only one in the town. I park and rush inside because I don't know how long they'll be open today. I'm surprised they're open at all. Half the shops are already boarded up except for this, the daycare, and the grocery store, which will soon abandon their open-for-twenty-four-hours motto in favor of an early night.

The bell rings overhead, and cool air rushes toward me as I walk into the building. The squat old man behind the desk checks his watch before greeting me.

"Can I help you?"

"Pick up for Knox Blakely."

The man rifles through garment bags, getting more furious with each passing bag. He better not have lost my suit. It's the only one I have. This night has a very strict dress code, and I don't have time to drive to another town to buy a suit. I'll be fucked if he can't find it.

"Is there a problem?" I ask.

"No, no, let me just check in back." The man leaves, returning with a tag in his hand. "It hasn't been pressed yet. If you want to wait outside, we'll have it done in ten or fifteen minutes."

I look at the clock above the desk and sigh. I have places to be, but I don't have any other options. I thank the man and head back outside to the departing sound of the bell.

I sit on the bench just outside the shop. My attention idles on the curling brown flowers that are slowly succumbing to fall's nighttime temperatures. They'll be spread across the ground in a few more days, but tonight is supposed to stay unusually warm, so they'll hold steadfast for one more night, at least.

The same can't be said for many of the town's occupants.

Wordless arguing infiltrates my ears, and I try to stop myself from turning toward the sound. It's not my business. But the argument grows more heated, and I finally look across the parking lot.

A couple stands beside a car. I can't hear what they're fighting about, but based on the guy's hostile body language, he's the most upset. He's got a short, blond, buzzed hairstyle and the most anger-soaked eyes I've ever seen. Especially looking at something as pretty as that girl.

I shake my head and try to ignore their spat, but a sudden motion draws my attention as the woman turns away from him. He rips her back by the hair and wraps the dark strands around his fist, then yanks her toward the ground. She falls with a scream, and I can't sit idle any longer.

I get up and make my way across the parking lot, then step between them to place my body in the path of his raised arm.

"Let's not," I say to the man.

"Mind your business!" he snarls.

"Oh, believe me, I fucking tried. But you made it my business when you manhandled her in fucking public." I reach down and offer my hand to her. She looks up at me with rich, dark eyes. I swear I see the hint of a bruise on her neck, and it pisses me off further.

"I'm fine. Sam didn't mean to knock me over," she says, clambering to her feet and brushing the dirt off her pants.

"*Sam* most definitely meant that," I say.

I put space between them as I usher her away from him. When he tries to follow me, I raise my fist at him. He recoils.

I stop and assess her. "Are you okay?"

She certainly doesn't look okay. Smears of makeup darken her cheeks as she forces a nod. "Yeah, we're fine."

"I didn't ask about him."

"I'm fine," she says, raising her chin.

She's the most stunning creature I've ever seen, and her stoic ways make her even more attractive. I very much understand that fake-it-until-you-make-it attitude. The feigned confidence. It's pretty much my eternal state at this point.

I turn my attention back to the sack of shit, who's grown enough balls to creep a little closer to us. "You're incredibly stupid. Pretty girl like that? Shit. Learn to do something better with your hands than abusing her."

I look back at her, and she wipes her cheeks to try to hide any sign of emotion, but I've done all I can at this point. I've already spent more time on their disturbance than I should have. If I don't get my suit before the dry cleaner panics and closes shop, I'm shit out of luck for the night.

Be careful, I mouth, and she throws me a quick, half-hearted nod.

I jog across the parking lot and make it back to the dry cleaners just as they turn their sign from Open to Closed. I go inside and pay the man before taking my suit to my car and stuffing it in the backseat.

My phone buzzes. I raise it, and the screen lights up as Adam's name flashes across the top.

Are you ready for tonight?

Of course I am. Pawns like me have true purpose tonight. I've been crafted into a killer and trained as their loyal attack dog. There was a time in the beginning when I was torn between being a good boy and ripping apart anything in front of me, but good no longer exists in me.

I study the text again. Adam was born into the Exodus. He's a pampered little shit stain, and I can't fucking stand him. In my position, however, I don't get to pick my friends. When Adam decided he wanted to be pals, I had to grin and pretend I wasn't dying inside.

He's not here to see my face as I climb into my car, so I don't have to fake the emotion with my body. My reply, however, needs to match his enthusiasm.

Hell yes!

I wipe my face and look into the rearview mirror. Life has been washed from my haunted gray eyes. Black hair falls over my forehead, but I blow it away on an exhale. I raise my sleeve as I stare at two dozen scars racing up and down my arm, crossing through my tattoos. I mark myself with pain after each slaying. Each scar represents a person I've killed since being turned into a henchman.

The self-inflicted cuts began as a prayer of apology to God, a way to put my emotional pain into a physical state. But the last few gashes? They were whispers of thanks to the devil. This is who I am now. The guilt is gone, which makes me feel like an animal instead of a human being.

That's what they've always wanted anyway. I'm the living embodiment of their goal. I'm their unquestioning killer.

The Exodus' hit list burns a hole in my pocket. The names of those they want eliminated during the ten-hour party. While they're fucking each other and having a grand time in the cabin, I'll do their dirty work and return to them with some kind of party favor.

A human taken against their will, much like I once was.

I make the drive back to my house, then head to my closet to make sure the entirety of my outfit is presentable. I'm not wearing a full suit; that's more common for the elders. Adam and I will likely wear the same thing: our suit pants and a black dress shirt. Black on black on black. Something that blends in with the night.

I pull the pressed slacks and shirt from the garment bag and hang them in my closet. My rabbit hops into my room and thumps his massive feet. He's a Flemish giant, and he has free range of my house. I reach down and stroke his dense black coat. He's dark enough to blend in with our outfits.

"Hey, Petey," I say as I rub his giant ears.

Call me a monster any other time of day, but I'm soft once you sit me down with this fucking animal. He was a meat rabbit, destined for slaughter, but I stole him from a pen at a farm, and I have zero regrets about it. God will shun me for everything I've done in the last decade, but maybe this rabbit and I can give him a little smile before he sends me off to hell.

"I'll be back late tonight. Don't wait up," I tell Petey, as if he can understand me.

I won't be home until after the ten-hour reckoning is over. Maybe later if I linger at the party so that I can fuck something other than my hand for a change.

I go and shower so I can wash off any guilt that may try to rear its ugly head. I'm not allowed to feel such things. It's a weakness—a sign that I'm failing at what my life has become. This monster is who I am now. There's no option to be someone else. There's no way to let the old me return. He's dead.

And I'm dead if I ever try to revive him.

CHAPTER 2

ALLISTER

Sam places his hand on my thigh as he steers the car down the street. Panic already pervades the town, and boards cover most store windows. Some have been completely abandoned in favor of a quick escape, and few shop owners still remain. I bear witness to the fear in their eyes as they furiously hammer nails into plywood.

The night from hell is coming.

No one knows exactly why it happens, but the townspeople share an understanding of the bare facts: you don't want to be on the streets on October tenth. You don't want to get caught outside on this night every decade. Horrific shit happens, and the police tell people nothing. Less than nothing. They claim it's a cult or a group of serial killers, but it's too chaotic. It's mayhem. I don't believe they know what's going on any more than we do.

But I know enough, which is more than some.

Ten years ago, I lost my father on this night. I was supposed to have the rest of my life with my dad, but he was taken from me when I was only ten years old. They—whoever *they* are—put nails through his feet, hands, and forehead. The worst part? The forehead shot didn't kill him. He'd stumbled back home so I could find him gurgling and wheezing on the porch stairs.

I was the one who pulled the nail from his head, though it took all the strength in my tiny body. Once I'd pulled the metal spindle free, blood poured down his face and the gurgling stopped. No one outright blamed me for my father's death, but the way the doctor looked at me after my mother spoke to him told me all I needed to know. The unknown assailants had driven the nails into him, but I had been the one to kill my father.

I was fucking ten. How was I supposed to know to leave the nail in place? There's not exactly a class or after-school special on what to do if your dad stumbles home with a six-inch bolt of metal through his skull. Regardless, none of it would have happened if these assholes—whoever they are—hadn't involved my father in their little crucifixion cosplay.

I stare at the mountains surrounding the town. Giant peaks that rise toward the sky and paint a picturesque scene. How does something so beautiful exist in such an ugly place?

I wipe away a tear and rip down the vanity mirror to assess the smudged makeup encasing my dark eyes. The green flecks throughout my irises were more visible when I was happy. It's been a long time since I've been happy. I ruffle my brown bangs, trying to bring some normalcy to my face.

"It's okay, Allister," Sam says as he gives my thigh a gentle squeeze. "We'll solve this tonight. We'll find out who they are."

Sam uses my full name, and when I'm thinking about my father, it holds more poignance. He named me after the little boy in *Wonder Woman*. Alistair. My mother complained it was a boy's name, and they compromised by calling me Allister, Alli for short. I wonder if any of them knew I'd one day make the same wish as the little boy in the movie.

"It's been a decade," I say. "Whoever comes out tonight probably won't be the same people who killed my father."

"It doesn't matter. If they're part of a system, they're *all* guilty. Look what they do to this town!" His hand reaches past me and gestures toward the deserted streets.

I want to agree with him, but even if we cut off the monster's legs, they'll just grow back. Until we can access the head of the beast, we're fighting a futile battle. Yet I still plan to wield a weapon and do as much damage as possible.

A few people meander up ahead, and I point to them. Don't they realize the severity of the situation? Why are they just milling about as if they have all the time in the world? We were out this way this morning, and it seems there are more people on the street now. They shouldn't linger.

And neither should we, but here we are.

Sam slows the car and pulls up beside a homeless man. He stands against a brick building, cupping a brown bag in his hands. Dirt encrusts his exposed skin, and his hair is a rat's nest of tangles and grime. Judging by the glassy look to his bloodshot eyes, he's three sheets to the wind already. He may not even realize the danger he's in.

I lower my window and lean toward him. "You have to go somewhere safe tonight!"

"What?" He cups the shell of his ear, squints, and tips the bottle against his mouth.

"It's October tenth, a decade since the last killing spree. It's not safe out here! You have to go somewhere tonight!" I raise my voice, almost yelling.

"Nowhere else for me to go." He takes another swig of whatever hides behind the thin brown paper, resigned to his fate.

"Shelters?" I ask.

"Full."

I look at Sam, but he just shrugs and begins to pull away from the curb. "You warned him. That's all you can do."

And it's not enough. This man will be dead by midnight, and I can't save him.

Panic begins to soak through me. I'm warning others to retreat to safety, yet I don't plan to heed my own advice. Sam and I are looking for danger instead of hiding from it, and we have our own murderous intent. We'll kill anyone who doesn't look afraid, though they'll be engulfed in fear by the time we finish with them.

I'm prepared to die for our cause, but I'll be damned if I don't take a few of those fuckers down with me first. If I can survive the night, even better.

It's the only way I can stop feeling this way. After ten years of guilt and misery over what happened, shedding their blood is the only thing that will make up for the loss of my father. I'll torture them like they tortured him, and then I'll leave them to gurgle on their daughter's doorstep.

I pull a knife from a sheath on my belt and run my finger along the blade. A sharp ache zips over my skin as the metal breaks through. Blood rises to the surface, leaving a red streak on the once immaculate metal.

Bringing my finger to my mouth, I let my tongue drift along my skin. The metallic tang hits my tongue and makes my eyes roll upward. I love it. And I'll love every drop I wring from whoever we catch tonight.

I sheathe the knife as Sam pulls the car into the driveway. We enter the house without speaking, both of us knowing we need to prepare for what's to come. I retreat to the bedroom and change into something dark.

When I walk into the living room, Sam is cleaning his pistol. Gaudy curtains hang in the windows, blocking any hint of outside light or life, but I know it's getting dark. That's why he's getting ready for tonight.

The mystery is what makes this so difficult. There's *something* going on, something more systematic than a cult or a serial killer, but we don't know who's involved. We've pored over news articles dating back at least half a century. Especially articles about my father's death.

Tragic accident took the life of Arthur Viot.

It wasn't a tragic fucking accident. It was murder.

Sam wipes his gun a final time and begins piecing it together again. He doesn't have the same passion for this as I do. He's into the idea of catching the people who torment the town every ten years, but he doesn't have a dog in the fight. No one he loves has been slain by these mysterious murderers. The vengeance I need is merely an afterthought for him. Unfortunately, that's not the only time I've been an afterthought.

It isn't that he doesn't fuck me anymore—the sex is constant—but he hasn't gotten me off in a year. Maybe longer. Eventually, I stopped keeping track of how long I've been in this dry spell. If I think about it too long, I'll be knocking on the door of deeper depression.

But the relationship woes extend far deeper than his lack of care for my pleasure. Like an evil tree with poisonous roots, the issues wrap around all that I am and hold me in place. The abuse started so subtly that I didn't notice what was happening until it was too late.

Sam pulls me onto his lap. "You ready, babe?"

"I've been ready for ten years," I say.

He kisses me, and I find myself thinking of anything besides his mouth on mine. A stranger's face fills my mind, and I almost recoil from Sam when I realize I'm thinking about that guy who got between us this morning. His dark and gray eyes. I wonder what it would have been like to kiss him . . .

Maybe after tonight, I can find the courage to tell Sam that this relationship has run its course. Maybe I can free myself from more than the torment I've endured since my father's death.

Thinking about the future is almost absurd, though. I'm under no illusions about what the night holds. What we've planned will be so risky. We could come face to face with something much bigger than we can handle on our own. But I *have* to try. It's kill or be killed tonight.

Historically, people on the streets are most at risk. College kids who don't know what's going on because schools don't want to scare away a big money maker on this side of Colorado. Sometimes the targets are people like my father, a man just coming home from work. Either way, they're killing innocent fucking people. Working people. I never see any rich people being knocked off on the sidewalk. The uppity women at the department stores who have a Mercedes waiting in the parking lot are nowhere to be found today.

It makes me wonder what they know that we don't.

I pick up Sam's pistol and flip the barrel toward the ceiling. "Let's go figure out who killed my father."

CHAPTER 3

KNOX

The rest of the day drags on, but I'm locked in hyper-focus every fucking minute. Once the sun sets, a clock ticks above my head. I sit on the porch and stare as the big yellow globe turns orange and sinks behind the horizon.

My phone chimes with a text from Adam.

T-1 hour!

Ready or not.

I pull the list from my pocket. After we make an appearance at the party and slide the masks over our faces, Adam and I will head out. The names on the list stare back at me. I've crossed off many already, leaving only the Granger family and the Robertsons.

It's time to put on my murderous attire. I'm not entirely sure why they require us to dress up. I hear the sex is wild there, so it seems like it would be better to wear fewer clothes, not all this extra fabric. I wouldn't know about the sex at the party, though. I was half dead when I was last on the property, and sex was the furthest thing from my mind at the time.

My fitted suit clings to every arm muscle, and a black dress shirt lies beneath the black pinstripe jacket. The collar is crisp and folded. I don't think I've ever looked this nice. Adam told me I couldn't come without my suit jacket, but I plan to take it off before we create joyous mayhem. Fair compromise, I guess.

With a spring to my step, I get into my car and head toward the mountains. I've never gone to the cabin when I wasn't under duress, and I don't even remember the winding roads or the massive trees that shield it. When I see a lake to the right, I know I'm getting close. Even though I was locked behind a curtain of exhaustion and fear, that body of water etched itself into my memory. The cabin sits partially suspended over the lake, which absorbs most of the screaming, leaving behind a peaceful silence.

My hand trembles as the scene from my memory materializes before me. My mind has tried to put that night behind me, but my body still remembers the pain and the hopelessness. It remembers the torture.

Hurt people hurt people. Isn't that the saying? They must have been hurting pretty bad, considering what they did to me. Now I hurt others in the most final form.

I park among a blanket of cars spread along the side of the cabin. From all external accounts, it looks like your average house party on the lake. But I know what waits inside, and when I walk up the cobblestone path to the entrance, breath struggles to escape my tightening throat.

A burly man in a suit meets me at the door. His hand goes up, and he stops me in my tracks. He doesn't say anything as he slides a wand behind me, hovering over the back of my neck. The device chimes and flashes green.

"Mr. Blakely," he says, and lets me inside.

Did they chip me? Does that mean they know where I am at all times? Or does it just tell them where I belong, like a lost fucking pet? Does that mean I'm home?

My hand wraps around the door handle, and I push open the door to a place that doesn't feel like home. I'm met with flashes of gold amid a tidal wave of black. A slim man in a black mask places a black wolf mask in my hands. Pawns—like me—and children of the elders wear black masks. The glinting gold face coverings belong to the elders.

Adam is an elder, and I wonder if he's among the people milling about in the middle of the room.

My attention catches on red ribbons, and, with my gaze, I follow the trail of aerial silk to the ceiling. Men and women twirl within the fabric, their bodies contorting and hanging in ways that seem impossible. I turn and spy a woman hanging upside down from the balcony railing. Her neck is split wide open, and her blood falls to a cascading tower of small glasses.

That could have been me ten years ago. An empty sacrifice for them to drink from.

I look up at the balcony, the second floor giving the gold masks a full view of the main floor. Someone leaps onto my back, his gold bird mask coming to rest beside mine.

"Hey, Knox!" he says, and I know that voice. It's Adam.

I inwardly cringe, but I know better than to show him my disdain. I clear my throat and muster a believable, "Hey!"

Adam struts in front of me, a proud peacock in a sea of suits. Nothing makes a born man feel more on top of the world than the night of the Reckoning. In his mind, I'm sure he's walking on water instead of the hardwoods beneath our feet. He's a god in his head.

He flips the mask over his face. The sharp downturn of the golden beak gives him an ominous look akin to those plague masks from the seventeenth century. "Are you ready for tonight?" he asks.

"I wouldn't be here if I wasn't."

He fists my shirt beneath my jacket and shakes me. It makes me want to sock him in the throat. He's so amped, and I can only assume he's been pre-gaming with something a little more hardcore than the liquor on offer. He verifies this as he steps back, pulls a bag of white powder from his pocket, and snorts a line off his hand.

"Take it easy there," I warn.

"Tonight is the night to do anything we want. Get high, fuck, kill. This place is fucking ours!" he says, his voice rising with every syllable until he's shouting at me. The arteries and veins in his neck strain against his thin skin. This dude's going to have a heart attack if he's not careful. "We are fucking gods, Knox!"

If by gods he means we decide who lives and dies, he's wrong. The names on this list are from the people who act as gods and decide who will be eliminated. If you serve no purpose in their estimation or if you dare to go against them, you end up on the list. Such fragile egos with these people.

Or maybe that's how they've maintained control for so long. Kill all threats to your secrecy. Get rid of any loose ends.

"We're gods tonight!" I say, though I don't feel much like one. I don't feel like I blend in with these people at all. But I'm not about to argue with his blasphemy.

I'll be what I truly am, though, and I'm no god. I'm a fallen angel, just like Lucifer.

"Come drink!" Adam motions me toward the bloody fountain.

We pull glasses from the tier, and I hope he doesn't see the hesitation in my movements. I'm not really into blood like they are. I don't believe it will infuse me with any kind of strength or power, and it doesn't provide good luck or whatever juju they believe in. But I take a swig with Adam because, despite not feeling like I'm part of them, I *am* part of them. And that means drinking up the sacrifice I almost became.

Full circle.

After I swallow the harsh, sticky, metallic liquid, Adam thrusts a beer against my chest. I gladly pop open the cap and take a sip to wash away the blood coating my mouth, then stare up at the lady above us. She's naked, her tits sagging toward the floor. Her throat hangs open like a gaping mouth, and blood still drips from the wound. She hasn't been dead long.

I wonder who brought this party favor? How many more are there tonight?

Turning to Adam, I raise my beer and take another swig. This woman won't be the only sacrifice. We're required to bring one of our own later.

The girl from this morning flashes into my mind. While I would love to see her again, I don't want to see her tonight. I protected her from the piece of shit who was beating on her, but I won't be able to protect her if Adam sets his sights on her. He likes to break pretty things, and if he sees her, I can almost guarantee he'll want to bring her in.

Hopefully, she's miles out of town by now. If not, she'd better have a very good hiding place.

CHAPTER 4

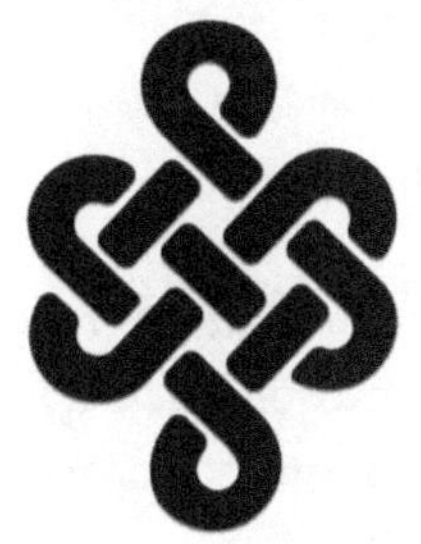

ALLISTER

Rough brick meets my palms as we take a moment to rest and listen. Running amongst the shadows is exhausting. I touch a bruise forming on my shoulder as I stare at Sam's back. I don't understand what I do to make him so angry. If I'm as terrible as he claims I am, why is he with me?

He knows why I'm with him. He caught me in his web when I was in the prime of my daddy-issues phase. And by daddy issues, I mean the fact that my daddy is dead. Abandonment issues of the most permanent kind. He used that to his advantage, securing me in silk until I couldn't leave.

I thought he wanted to take care of me, but he was only ensuring I had no finances with which to leave him. I believed he loved me, but I now know that he only loves two things: himself and control. Now . . . I'm stuck.

A scream breaks through the quiet, coming from the other side of the building we're hunkered down behind. I look around for somewhere better to hide. A rusty dumpster stands in the alleyway, and when I look back at Sam, he nods. We rush for it as the screams grow closer.

I peel back the lid and shudder at the mingling, fetid scents of decaying food matter, sour milk, and piss concentrate. Looking back toward the source of the sounds, I consider the alternative to diving face first into this cesspool, but the screams have become noisy footsteps.

And they're drawing closer.

Fuck.

I heave myself over the side of the dumpster, and my feet sink into squishy mounds of black trash bags filled with god knows what. I get caught on the corner of one and rip the bag, soaking my pants in stale coffee.

Gross, I think, but I don't have time to focus on hygiene as Sam lands next to me. He holds the lid and eases it closed, enfolding us in a deeper darkness as we hide and hope for the best.

As the seconds pass and the adrenaline wanes, the fragrant scent of garbage overtakes my senses. The smells wrap my lungs in a chokehold, squeezing until I'm certain I'll suffocate on a throne of dirty diapers and vegetable peelings. I grip Sam's sleeve. Between the cloying perfume and the panic, I almost want to leap out and throw myself into the unknown.

When I can't take it anymore, I make a move to get up. My head touches the metal lid, but Sam pulls me down, forcing my ass onto another bag of trash.

"Stop," he whispers.

I wish he were trying to protect me, but those delusions are long gone. He's simply trying to save his own ass. If they find *me*, they find *him*.

Sound explodes just outside the dumpster. I put my hand over my mouth to silence a startled shout. A man screams, and then the sound of squelching flesh reaches my ears.

Everything in me wants to jump out and help the man, but not this way. We can't. We need to have the upper hand, and there's no place lower than the fucking garbage. My heart breaks for the stranger who will likely die just feet away from our hiding place.

"Please . . . don't," he whispers. Wet sounds punctuate the ragged breath between each word.

His attacker feels no pity. He only laughs. He's toying with him.

The sounds bring me right back to the moment with my father. Had he begged for his life to be spared? Had his pain and agony brought his tormentor as much joy?

My heart aches, and I have to fight the urge in my muscles to get up and stop this, whatever it is, but before I can move again, the pleading stops. Everything stops.

Footsteps near the dumpster, and the lid opens. We make ourselves as small as possible and pray the killer doesn't see us. Moonlight shines through the crack as he tosses something into the heaps of trash. It lands in my lap. Imagine my surprise when I look down and see a man's head.

His mouth, frozen in death's grip, twists in agony. Heavy lids hang over his unseeing eyes. Warm blood drips from the gaping neck stump and mixes with the coffee permeating my jeans.

I clap my hand over my mouth again, my nostrils flaring as I try to keep the human guillotine from hearing me.

Don't move, Sam mouths.

Sweat pours down my temples and makes my face itch. I don't move a muscle, though. My need to keep my head firmly attached to the rest of me overrides the urge to scratch.

The dumpster slams shut, and the man outside begins to whistle as he walks away. The footsteps recede, slow and unbothered, as if he didn't just kill a man and toss his head into my fucking lap. Once the footsteps become a distant memory, I let out a breath and push the head away from me. I can't take another second of staring into his terrified face.

"Oh god," I whisper, the words choking out of me.

"Quit bitching. You're fine," Sam whispers.

"But *he's* not," I say, gesturing toward the severed head.

"As long as it's not us."

That's where Sam and I differ, I guess. He doesn't care as long as it's not us. I don't want it to be anyone ever again.

Sam cracks the lid and peers out of the opening. When he's satisfied the coast is clear, he lifts the lid off the rest of the way. He climbs up, balancing on the rim, then hops out of the dumpster. I go to do the same, but Sam's voice breaks through the silence.

"You might not want to look," he says.

"I need to look."

The man's body lies in a widening puddle of blood on the concrete. His neck is a mess of red flesh and white bone, and a large cut runs from his sternum to his pelvis. Pink organs peek through the gash.

I wish I was more nauseated or frightened by what I'm seeing, but it just makes me angry. This man's death heats my blood until it's burning me from the inside.

"Who would do this?" I whisper.

"Monsters."

"No. Even monsters are more humane than this."

"Let's figure out who they are, then."

I nod and step over the body, but I can't stop myself from wondering if he has a daughter. If so, will she grow up and seek vengeance as I have?

If Sam and I can put an end to this nightmare, maybe she won't have to.

We step into the shadows and continue on.

CHAPTER 5

KNOX

Alcohol courses through my veins. How did one beer turn to three? Or maybe it was four? I've lost count.

A woman dances in front of me. Her seductive blue eyes peer out from behind the holes in her black mask. She beckons me over with a curl of her manicured finger, and I want to join her. Believe me, I want to.

But I have a job to do.

I also can't seem to shake off the lingering mental image of the girl I met this morning. None of the nearly bare bodies before me compare to the mystery of what waited under her clothes. How has one brief encounter left me so obsessed?

I shake my head and drift to the edge of the room. Reclining against the wooden wall, I watch the others. Women in various stages of undress dance around the men. My gaze snags on a blonde woman whose dress straps have fallen, allowing the fabric to bunch beneath her large, fake tits. Another blonde wiggles close by, bent at the waist as she gyrates her ample ass in a hypnotizing display. Her short cock-tail dress rides up her thighs.

You couldn't cut the sexual tension in this room with the sharpest knife. The air is electrified.

When I turn to the left, I spot a couple fucking on a glass table. The woman's arms extend above her head, a beautiful arch in her back as the masked man rails her. I home in on the moans coming from her lips and adjust the front of my pants, hoping no one notices my erection. But it isn't her voice I hear. Not really. I hear the girl from this morning.

I need to find some place in this house to rub one out before Adam comes back from wherever he's disappeared to.

I head toward a door and ease it open, revealing a dark room with strips of black lights overhead. Bodies rub against each other everywhere I look. Neon paint coats their skin. Sensual music plays overhead, a direct contrast with the livelier music in the main hall. Everyone is naked and some are fucking, heads dropped back as if they're on the best trip of their lives. Some still wear masks, but others have discarded them in the corner. A few may not have had a mask at all.

The maskless will face the ultimate choice, much as I did all those years ago, but I wish I'd gotten this kind of treatment back then. Where was this kind of party welcoming me into this place? I didn't get my rocks off before I made the decision to live for them or die for me.

I hide in the shadows and unzip my slacks. This isn't my first choice of a quiet place to beat my dick, but the visuals are good. If I use my imagination, I can almost imagine some of these masked individuals are me and my mystery girl.

My cock springs from the fabric, and I wrap my hand around it, grazing the two surface piercings along the top of my shaft. A modified Jacob's ladder. There aren't as many rungs and it looks like I chickened out, but I didn't. This was by design. I wanted it to rake the woman's pussy when I'm in my favorite position, which is over her, owning her.

I stroke myself to the dark, artsy motions. Moans overtake

the room, drowning out the music. I bring my hand to my mouth and spit before wrapping it around my dick once more. I drop my head back and moan as the pleasure moves from my balls to the head of my cock.

In my mind, it's the girl bringing me all this pleasure. On her knees. Bent over the back of the couch with her ass in the air. Lying down as she arches her back and comes on my cock. She's beautiful perfection, each moan a musical note that draws the pleasure out of me.

I don't hold it back or try to catch it as I bust. White ropes of come splash across the dark floor and mix with droplets of bright-yellow paint. The best part? It fucking glows beneath the black light.

A woman who looks high on something delightful crawls to my feet and looks up at me before dropping her face to the ground and licking up some of my come.

"Thank you," she says with a smirk as she wipes her chin.

I stare at her paint-covered body as she stands. Her nipples are hidden by a streak of pink, but it only enhances the curves of her breasts. She walks off and goes back to enjoy the party. This might have tempted me yesterday, but now I'm too wrapped up in a woman I'll never see again. Which is probably for the best. I need to focus.

I tuck myself away, zip my pants, and head back to the main party. I walk right into Adam, who looks very annoyed.

"We gotta get going!" He gestures toward the door.

"I've been waiting for you," I remind him as we head toward the entrance.

Once we're outside, Adam gets in the driver's seat of his Cadillac, and we start down the driveway. I worry he'll wrap us around a tree with the way he's driving, but there's nothing I can do about it now. We have to get to the center of town, so I just grip the oh-shit handle and try to downplay my anxiety.

Before we can enjoy our own murderous inclinations, we

have to take care of the remaining names on our list. First up is a family. They don't live in the town center, so we're forced to make a slight detour.

Adam pulls the car to a stop at the base of a long, twisty driveway. The Arlows were part of the society, but the father and mother decided they no longer wanted to participate. Unfortunately, none of us can decide that.

We get out of the car, and Adam heads to the trunk. He pulls two pistols from inside and hands one to me. Next, he picks up a metal bat for himself before placing an ice pick in my palm. I already have a knife tucked down the back of my waistband, but more torture tools are always better.

After abandoning the car, we cross the massive lawn. Dew transfers from the lush grass to my shoes and soaks through my socks. Lovely. Adam spots several cameras, then swats them with the bat to disable them.

We're met with a roadblock at the front door. Wide iron bars attached to a solid frame prevent us from getting inside. Rich people have such luxury.

Undeterred, we head toward the back of the house, but the same metal bars obscure every entrance. Even the windows are covered in iron. Luckily for us, they missed the small window leading into the basement.

I use the ice pick to shatter the glass. It's a tight fit, but both of us make it through after a bit of wiggling and a few curse words muttered under our breath. Once inside, it's cake to break through the basement door and enter the main areas of the house.

The Arlows are understandably freaked out by the time we make it up the stairs. Their panic likely began as soon as the cameras went out.

"Oh god," Mr. Arlow says, clutching his wife and daughter to him.

"Yes," Adam says, a creepy smile crossing his face. "I am God."

Mr. Arlow pulls a small pistol from behind his back, but Adam isn't afraid to call his bluff. He draws his handgun and sends one well-aimed bullet into Mr. Arlow's gut. His family screams, and both his wife and daughter move away from him as if they've been shot as well. Blood oozes from the small hole in his nightshirt as red begins to spread through the material. His wife leans forward and tries to hold pressure to the wound, soaking her hand in crimson.

"The Exodus sends their regards," Adam says.

Mrs. Arlow grips her dying husband's shirt and stares into his wide eyes. "I thought you said they approved of us leaving?"

Mr. Arlow shakes his head. "I didn't think they'd do this. I've invested so much into them, Janet. I thought I'd earned my peace."

"Let's see how peaceful you feel while I fuck your wife in front of you," Adam snarls, ripping the woman away from her husband.

"No, please!" she screams.

Adam wrestles her to the couch as the daughter rushes forward and grabs the back of Adam's shirt, crying for her mother and begging him to release her.

"Take care of the kid!" Adam yells.

I don't enjoy the thought of watching what Adam plans to do to this woman, but it would be better than killing a kid. Unfortunately, no isn't an answer here. Not with them. Not even if I invested all my money in the society like this sad sap.

I grab the kid by the shoulder and rip her away from Adam so he can be Adam. She kicks and screams, catching me several times in the shin, but I won't be deterred. I drag her into their massive kitchen.

When she sees the ice pick in my hand, she goes to bite me.

I look into her dark eyes and discover a strength I can't help but envy. She's a fighter.

"Shut the fuck up." I grip her hair and crank back her neck.

"Let me go, ugly face!"

I raise the ice pick with my free hand and aim it at her, but my resolve weakens. I lean toward her ear, trying to speak to her, but she tries to bite me. There's no getting through to her when she's in this state of panic, so I strike the pick forward and cut a hole in her nightgown to snap her out of it.

She screams.

"Listen to me, listen to me!" I whisper, and she stops flailing. I roll up my sleeve and cut into my arm. Blood pools to the surface, and I wipe a hand through it and coat the front of her gown. Then I hold the fresh wound over her and let it saturate her skin. "Scream again, little girl, and make it believable."

"What?" she asks, her lips pursed in disgust at what I've just done.

"I need you to scream like I'm killing you. And then you have to play dead. Okay? Just lie here and play pretend. But you can't move. Not a muscle."

She nods and screams. I smash the pick against the floor, and she throws herself to the ground. I drip blood into her dark-blonde hair and mess it up. I hit the pick against the island, put my finger to my lips, and shush her.

Play dead, I mouth.

I'm being weak, but I don't want to kill that little girl.

My head whips backward when I hear the pained sounds coming from the mother in the living room. I wrap my arm in a thin towel, then lower my sleeve to conceal the self-inflicted injury. I don't need to hide it too well, though. Adam knows I cut myself each time I kill.

I kneel over the girl and cover her ears with both hands to

keep her from hearing the sounds of her mother being railed by "God." Her screams and Adam's groans filter through the wall. When they stop, I release her ears and see tears streaming down her face. I wipe them away.

"What's your name?" I ask.

"Rosa," she whispers.

"I'm sorry, Rosa. Be good and keep playing dead."

She lies back and closes her eyes.

I stand up just as Adam crashes into the kitchen, still zipping up his pants. He looks down at the girl, and I can't mistake the moment of question on his face for anything else. He's suspicious.

"Do you have any more coke?" I ask, trying to pull him away from looking too hard at her.

"In the car. She's good?"

"Dead."

"Sick fuck. You hardly fought me at all on killing a kid." He laughs, and I consider strangling him right here. But the girl has seen enough.

"It's all done in there?"

"Yup," he says with a smile. "Let's go get higher."

We can get as high as we want, but it won't raise me from the depths of depravity I've fallen into.

CHAPTER 6

ALLISTER

I'm covered in blood and spoiled coffee. I look insane right now, but I guess that's a good look for what we plan on doing. As Sam drags me down another deserted road, my heart thumps against my chest. We could run into someone at any moment, and there are no buildings or alleyways to hide us now. I said we should stay back and wait, but Sam thinks we have a better chance of finding someone closer to the town's center.

I trip and fall forward, my wrists skidding along the cobblestone path. It's my favorite thing about the town, and now my blood is staining the ancient stones.

"Come on, get up!" Sam says in a harsh whisper. His head swivels in all directions, scanning the open space for anyone.

We really are sitting ducks right here.

I climb to my knees and scramble back to my feet. We take off toward the shops, but I stop mid-step as we reach the strip of stores. The word "traitor" has been scrawled on the brick in black paint. My eyes slowly rise to find a man hanging above it.

His body swings listlessly, and it looks like he was tossed from the roof.

Which means they've been here.

I'm tempted to tell Sam never mind, that we should just go home, but then my father flashes into my mind again. I remember how he looked, slumped on our front porch. I hardly recall pulling the nail from his skull, but the memory of the blood pouring in a thick line down his face burns brightly. So does the blood coating his eyes as he cried. And the way crimson ribbons poured from his mouth before his head dropped back.

These painful memories remind me why I'm doing this. This is my only chance for another decade, and I can't miss it. I *can't.*

"Get your shit together. They've already been here, and we're out in the open!" Sam yells, but his voice sounds so far away.

I'm guessing the grim memories have frozen me in place and left me lost in a time I don't want to live in any longer. My body shakes, and that drags me from my mind and sets me back in the middle of the street. I look around, orienting myself. He's right, we have to get going, and fast.

Because footsteps are running toward us now.

We both look at each other with similar panic in our eyes. Sam grabs my arm and pulls me around the corner and to the front of the building. I peer past the edge and see a man in a suit. He raises a metal bat and swings it against another man's head. The hollow *thunk* as metal collides with bone is a sound I won't soon forget.

When I catch a glimpse of the man on the ground, I recognize him as the homeless man from earlier. His head is split open, falling apart in two distinct segments, but his hands keep moving, reaching toward his assailant. He's fucking alive.

Oh god.

I throw my hand over my mouth to suppress the agonizing scream twisting through my throat. Tears stream down my face in thick lines. I mumble words beneath my hand, and Sam slaps at the back of it.

"I can't understand you," he whispers.

"The man . . . the homeless guy. His head . . ."

"Wait, you saw them? Who did it?"

"There are two men. One is wearing a suit, and the other is missing his jacket. But Sam, the homeless guy is still alive."

"There's nothing we can do for him, Alli."

"We can't leave him."

"We have to. Come on."

"No!"

"You cannot help that man. Stop being stubborn. Come on!" He stands, grips my hand, and tries to haul me away, but I won't be moved.

Anger brews inside me and replaces my absolute fear. I pull the pistol from my waistband and cradle it in my lap.

"Don't even fucking think about it," Sam warns.

Oh, I'm thinking about it.

"You know what?" he says. "Get yourself killed, then. I don't care."

He takes off down the road.

Thanks, dude.

I grab my phone and dial 911, but a robotic voice tells me the line is out of service. How? It's fucking 911.

If no help is coming, I need to put the man out of his misery. It's the least I can do. I can't listen to the sound of him dying for a moment longer.

I step into the road and fight the urge to aim my pistol at the poor man on the ground, whose eye hangs out of one half of his head. His hand still moves on his lap, and my heart breaks.

"Hands up, asshole," I say to the man in front of me. A

black wolf mask covers his face. My eyes scan around me, trying to find the guy with the bat, but I don't see him.

"What do you want?" the man says, raising his hands in the air. An ice pick balances between his fingers.

"What you goddamn pussies wouldn't do," I say as I step sideways, keeping my pistol on him. I draw the knife from my hip and sink the blade into the side of the homeless man's neck. When I yank the blade away, a red jet squirts onto the cobblestone path.

"Unless you want to draw attention of all of us, I don't think you'll fire that weapon," the masked man says.

"If that didn't show you that I can kill a man, I don't know what will," I say. "How many of you are there?"

As he cocks his head, I can almost see his smirk behind the mask.

Footsteps encroach from the left, and the man with the bat appears from the shadows. A gold bird mask covers his features. As soon as he sees what he's walked in on, he lowers the bat to his side.

"Don't fucking move or I'll rearrange your face with a bullet," I say as I aim my gun at him.

"Shoot her, Knox!" the gold mask says. An uncomfortable laugh follows his words. He steps closer to the black-masked man and points the bat at me. "Kill that bitch!"

Only then do I notice the pistol in wolf mask's—Knox's—waistband.

CHAPTER 7

KNOX

Why do I have the worst luck? The girl with the gun is the same girl from the parking lot. If I didn't have my mask on, she'd see the recognition all over my face.

Where was this spunk when her piece-of-shit boyfriend knocked her to the ground earlier? Maybe she ended up getting rid of him and doing a bit of reckless killing on her own. Regardless, I won't shoot this woman if I can avoid it. She's been through enough as it is, though she doesn't look nearly as helpless now as she did this morning. She looks terrifying. Like she should be dressed up and on our side.

I go for my pistol, but she moves the barrel from Adam to me. It's fucking hot. But it's also a little scary. Fire licks within her dark irises, as if killing us will solve some age-old curse upon her.

This is not how this night is supposed to go. They aren't supposed to have the upper hand. Ever. They're sheep for slaughter. But not this girl. She appears to be a wolf in sheepskin.

"Let's talk about this," I say, raising my hands.

"No." She lowers the pistol a bit as she speaks. "I don't want to talk about it. I've talked about it enough."

Maybe she'll speed up the process and kill me now. I fucked up at that house we just came from. I left the daughter alive, and that will get back to the elders. It was an unfinished job, unworthy of the bloody streak across their name, and I'll certainly have to pay for it.

Movement catches my attention, and I see that Adam decided to take a chance when he saw her lower the barrel a bit. He catches her beneath her arms, and they fight for the pistol as they drop to the ground. He rolls on top of her, pinning her body beneath his, then rips the pistol from her and flings it out of reach.

"No, let me go, asshole!" she yells.

A smirk creeps across my face, and I wish she could see it, but if she looked hard enough, she'd see just how hard she makes me. Watching her strain and writhe beneath him isn't helping. But then I hear a belt coming undone and the brush of denim as he tries to pull her jeans down her ass.

Well, fuck.

I didn't want to watch him assault that lady, and I don't want to watch him assault this one. Especially since my body seems to have laid a claim on her already. I look beyond them. It's a great time to escape them both.

But then my eyes find hers. She looks up at me with eyes that beg for me to do something. Anything. I run over to them, my actions fueled by her whimpers.

Again, I could run. I *should* run. This bitch will draw a gun on me the moment she's free. But I sigh, draw my arm back, and send the ice pick into Adam's spine. He's still squirming, so I pull it out and drive it in twice more. It's a quick way to end his assault, but I don't know who I'm doing this for. Is it so that I can escape or so that I can save the girl?

His legs go flaccid, and he falls forward onto her. He

desperately tries to scoot away with his arms, dragging them along the rough cobblestones, but he only pulls himself further up her body. He raises his hand to rip off his mask, but it falls beside him.

Blood rises and flows in a cascade from his lower lip to her bare forearms. I must have nicked his lung when I drove the ice pick into his back the second or third time. She whines with an almost annoyed sound that makes me chuckle as Adam flails like a fish on top of her.

Sorry this is such an inconvenience, pretty girl.

"Get this fuck off me!" she squeals beneath him.

I pull the ice pick out of his back, spilling more blood as I kick him off her. The moment he's rolled over, I see that her panties and jeans are down to her upper thighs. I don't know if he actually got to her or not. Either way, it was too close.

I catch myself staring at the curve of her exposed ass as she rushes to pull up her pants. I step on her gun, then pick it up and put it beside mine before looking into Adam's widened eyes.

I've been in his shadow for a decade. He brought me to the party initially, and I became his made man. He owned me. And now I'm standing over his mortally wounded body. Again, this is *not* how this night was supposed to go.

"I know there will be an inside trial for me over this, but if I get sentenced to death, at least I took you with me," I say to him.

"Don't," he sputters.

I raise the ice pick, and as I arc for his head, the woman on the ground sits up on her knees, screaming for me to stay my hand.

"Let him suffer longer," she says, her eyes fixated on Adam. She's glowing over it.

I kill because I have to. Because it's my job. She's looking at it like it's a whole-ass hobby. Something enjoyable. Even so, it makes me stop mid-swing, and I lower the ice pick to my side.

I balance the pick between my fingers and hold it toward the girl. "Do you want the honors?"

This is stupid. I'm being stupid. But I have a gun. Two of them, actually. I reach over and take the pistol from Adam, and that makes three ballistic weapons against a measly ice pick.

Her eyes leap to mine before landing on the bloodied weapon in my hand. She's drooling over the prospect. There's such a desire in her eyes that I think she'd suck my dick for the chance to kill Adam.

I'm tempted to ask.

Instead, I toss the weapon toward her. She grabs it by the handle and looks at me as she stands up, as if she fears I'll rescind my offer at any moment. I won't. I like how she skulks over to him like some predator that's just learning she has the teeth and claws to kill. She's already killed, but that man was suffering. He was innocent. This is different.

"What's your name?" I ask before she can kill him. I should have asked her in the parking lot, but I didn't. Now I want to know what this beautiful beast is called.

"Why does it matter?"

"If I were him, I'd sure like to know the name of the woman about to end my life."

"He'll learn my name in hell. And so will you!" she says. "Call me your karma."

She raises the ice pick and stabs it into his left hand, then the right. Adam's screams rejuvenate the night. She stabs into his eye socket next, and the screams stop.

Now I need to figure out what I'll tell the others. Killing an elder is certain death.

Oh no, Adam and I were ambushed. He was killed.

The story works for me, but will it work for them? I'll find out soon enough.

I stare at the back of Miss Karma's head as I back away. When I've put some distance between us, I take off toward the car. I make it half a block before I'm speared to the ground, disoriented as fuck. There's no way the girl caught up to me, nor would she have the strength to take me out like this.

My side scrapes against the cobblestone pathway as we roll to the ground. I reach back for my pistol—any one of them—but a hand wraps around my wrist and presses my arm against my back, holding me in place. The hold reminds me of something. The police? They'd never. The Exodus has a wide berth of immunity and protection.

So who the fuck has me? And why?

CHAPTER 8

ALLISTER

"Sam!" I say as I run toward him. "You came back for me." I'm glad to see him, but I'm equally surprised he didn't leave me to my own devices. I curse myself for being happy to see him at all. He fucking left me to deal with two armed men on my own. Would he have cared if I died?

He's pinned the man beneath him. He grabs my pistol from his waistband and throws it toward me, and I aim it at the stranger.

"I knew you'd get into trouble here." He shoves his chin toward me, then reaches down and grabs the other two pistols, tossing them at my feet. "You're unarmed, dickhead."

"Then kill me already," Knox snarls.

"That will happen soon enough. When you're begging for death," I say. I pluck handcuffs from my belt and help Sam restrain him.

"You're kidnapping me?" Knox asks.

"Bit too old to be kidnapped," I say with a smirk as I squat in front of him.

His masculine scent rises to my nose, and I'm suddenly

aware of every rippling muscle beneath his dress shirt. Messy, dark hair falls over his mask, but I want to see his face. I rip the mask away, revealing haunting gray eyes.

He's the man from the parking lot. The one who stepped between me and Sam.

The humanity beneath the mask catches me off guard. How could he have been a kind person mere hours ago, then turn into a savage who kills defenseless homeless people? He looks normal. Handsome, even. He doesn't look like a monster or have some grotesque disfigurement he's hiding beneath the latex and plastic.

But if they aren't monsters beneath masks, how could they have done such a horrible thing to my father?

My eyes scan Sam's face for signs of recognition, but I see nothing. How could he forget the face of someone who got between us to keep him from punching me? How much did that rage blind him?

Knox's eyes roll up to mine.

"Hello, karma," he whispers.

A chill rakes my spine. We both recognize each other now. That's very clear.

Hello. Karma.

We get him up on his feet and walk him toward the alley. I'm surprised he hasn't yelled for his friends, since I'm sure there are more of them. Without a peep, he walks with his arms behind his back and his gaze on the ground.

After a while, Sam pulls ahead of us. I keep glancing at the man. I still can't believe it's the same guy.

"I should have let him do what he does best," he whispers beside me.

"You're right. And you probably should have run." I'm glad he didn't, in a way, but he should have taken off when he had the chance.

"Curse my conscience," he says.

"If you had one of those," I say, "you wouldn't be out here."

"You're out here, aren't you?" he says, his gray eyes forcing their way into mine.

I tighten my lips. We're not the same. I'm trying to protect people!

A little voice in my head hums.

No, you want vengeance.

No, I want both.

A piece of me wants to give him grace for stopping Sam's attack on me this morning, then stopping his friend tonight. My mind clouds with ideas of how him being out there has to be a mistake. Someone can't be kind and horrible at the same time. But wolves don't always attack, and that doesn't make them any less dangerous.

This man is a part of whatever larger organization altered my brain chemistry with what they did to my father. His momentary kindness doesn't negate what needs to be done. It can't.

After I force as much information as I can out of him, then kill him, I will have avenged my father's death the best way I could. In the only way I know how. An act of violence shaped my teenage years. It was in the back of my mind every single day as I grew up. It's a ball of negativity, growing and darkening inside me. It's why I could kill the man who was suffering. It's why I could kill Knox's rapey fucking friend.

But it wasn't enough torture for me or my dad. And that's where this guy comes in.

The need for revenge meets opportunity.

CHAPTER 9

KNOX

I wake up chained in a bedroom. Smacking my dry lips, I try to pull some moisture from beneath my tongue. I must have been drugged. I remember telling that girl I should have let Adam do what he planned to do, but then I remember nothing else. A warm feeling coats my mouth. Did they fucking chloroform me?

I look around the room. I'm handcuffed to the bed's metal footboard. The room's warmth causes my balls to stick to my thigh. A night light emits a blue glow from the corner and leaves a similar hue dancing across my skin.

My skin? Why am I shirtless? Why am I *naked*? And where the fuck am I?

All I can think about is Petey. Luckily, I left him with extra food and water in case I ran late after the party. Or if, god forbid, I ended up dead at the party, because you never truly know with them.

Karma comes into the room, eyeing me and my testicular glory. I've never been an insecure man, but there's something humbling about your naked human form chained up on the floor. No matter how good you think you look, that goes away in this position. Nothing sexy about a limp dick resting on a pair of nuts.

She's so superior to me right now, and she's looking down at me like she knows it. It's fucking hot.

Stop thinking she's hot. She abducted you.

She'd look pretty chained up on the floor. Naked. Her tight little slit resting on the old hardwoods. Maybe she'd leave the wood nice and wet afterward. Well, that thought takes care of my limp-dick problem. And I wish it wouldn't.

I put my arm over my erection. She doesn't need any more of my power.

"What do you want, karma?" I ask, raising my hardened stare to her face. "Or why don't you tell me your real name? I know you recognize me because I recognize you."

"I'm not telling you anything about me."

"That little interaction in the parking lot told me enough to know that you're letting some asshole who doesn't deserve you make you into this—"

"He isn't making me into anything. This is *my* choice. I appreciate what you did in the parking lot and that you didn't shoot me when you had the chance, but it doesn't change *anything.*"

"Don't make me regret my decision to let you live. What. Do. You. Want?" I'm losing patience with her.

"I want you to spill your guts about whatever this is." She gestures toward the black wolf mask sitting on top of my clothes.

I can't give her what she wants, though. That info is well guarded. Anyone caught sharing anything about the Exodus ends up on a list like mine.

My list.

I look at my clothes again. Where is it? Has she seen it? I wish I could tell her I'm just a pawn, nothing more and everything less, but that list, with its bloody, crossed-out names, makes me look like more than what I am.

"I can't," I say.

She walks over, lifts her heel, and stomps down on my cock and balls. "How about now?"

I open my mouth in a soundless scream as pain rushes to my lap and seems to work its way through every muscle in my body. "No," I choke out.

She twists her heel. "I don't care if I crush your dick."

"I think you do care . . . based on the way you look at it."

"Fuck you." She digs her heel into me, mashing the most sensitive area on my body.

Fuck, that hurts.

"I don't know what I did to you, but can you not take it out on my dick?" I grip her ankle with my free hand to take the pressure off my junk. "Girl, can we not?"

"Oh, does that hurt?"

"Listen, I have a son at home. You have to let me go," I say. Petey *is* my son. I'd burn the world down for that rabbit.

"I don't care."

She finally pulls her foot off my dick, which unfortunately hurts a lot worse because it was hard. For her. Stupidly for her. There's a mark where her heel has bruised my flesh.

"So you really aren't going to talk?" she asks. "This only gets worse from here."

My dick and I both wish I could, but if I tell her anything, we're as good as dead. They'll send someone like me to take care of us.

"No, I can't."

A frustrated exhale leaves her full lips. When she takes a step back and brushes her face with the back of her hand, she smears her makeup. A hint of discoloration circles her right eye.

"What's that bruise from?" I ask, trying to take her attention off me.

Her lips tighten. "Nothing."

"Well, something bruised you. Did he hurt you again?"

"You don't get to ask me questions! This isn't how this works!" she says.

Hey, I said the same thing. None of this is how this works. She should be fucking dead. Or even better, she should be my party favor. She'd look pretty as she begs for her life. To be honest, this girl would look pretty doing just about anything. With her dark hair pulled back in the messy ponytail, she looks somehow elegant and sloppy, but firmly sexy. She looks as if she'd kill me with a smile on her face. Possibly with my severed dick in her hand. Who knows what this kinky bitch is into.

"Listen, just let me go. I have a party I absolutely cannot miss." I strain and look at the digital clock beneath the television. "In four hours."

"A party? A fucking party!" she says with an angry laugh. "This is a night of partying for you?"

"For people beyond me. That's what you don't seem to understand. I'm a cog, karma."

"Stop calling me that."

"That's what you told my friend, isn't it?" I ask.

Was Adam really my friend, though? Nah, more like my handler.

"*Call me karma.*" I repeat her words back to her, and she looks at me like she wants to tap dance on my balls again.

"You just wait, *Knox.*" She calls me by my name, which Adam used like a fucking idiot. I go to argue that it's not my real name, but then I look over at my discarded pants and realize she probably has my ID anyway. We're supposed to leave identification at home, so I fucked that up.

"What am I waiting for, exactly?" I ask.

"For *your* karma."

CHAPTER 10

ALLISTER

After drugging him again, I retreated to my bedroom to compose myself. A white stuffed rabbit sits on the bed. One of its eyeballs hangs by a literal thread, and its coat is dirty and ragged, but it's soothed me to sleep more times than I can count. It was a gift from my father.

I stare at myself in the mirror as I swipe concealer across my cheek and around my eye. The bruises disappear beneath the thick cover-up. My hand crawls over the bruises I've hidden beneath my clothes.

I can't believe that guy noticed the mark on my face. And how dare he ask about it. It's not his business. It's no one's business but mine and Sam's.

I shake my head because we made it his business when we fought in public. Sam very much made it his business when he went to punch me again. It's the first time the abuse has been witnessed by someone else, which means it's escalating. Sam doesn't care who sees him hit me now.

Brushing over my skin once more, I force my weakness aside. Knox shouldn't have looked at me with some kind of pity, especially when he couldn't spare a drop of it for that dying man. He's clearly hardened to suffering, so he shouldn't look at me like I need anyone's help.

I don't need help from anyone, least of all him. Sam has always taken out his frustrations on me, though it's never been this bad. When he hits me, I want to leave him, but then the Sam I know comes back and rocks me to sleep and tells me he's sorry and that he'll never do it again. Rinse and repeat.

I wouldn't have gotten Knox chained up in the guest bedroom without him, though. I'm desperate to get the information I need out of him, and this is my only chance.

I twist my hair into a bun and head into the guest room. An overturned mug sits beside him, spilling a little bit of the liquid onto the wooden floorboards. My eyes crawl over his naked body. Hardened muscles ripple under his skin, and his limp dick rests against his leg. Even flaccid, it's impressive, especially once I notice two sets of black metal balls about three-fourths of the way down his shaft. I've never seen a man with a pierced cock in real life, let alone two piercings.

I grab the jug Sam gave him to pee in and empty it out in the bathroom, then set it down beside him. After plucking the hammer and nails off the dresser, I kneel in front of him. His head hangs low, full lips set in a relaxed expression. Dark hair falls over his face, and haunting gray eyes hide behind his closed eyelids.

My hand moves without my permission and reaches for his dick. I graze the warm skin resting against his leg. He feels like velvet.

I rip my hand away when he hardens beneath my touch. I didn't expect the movement. The tightening skin. The beast that it transformed into. My jaw loosens, letting my lower lip fall.

Then I remember what sits before me. These people are monsters, and I shouldn't even be looking at his erection, but there's something oddly vindicating about holding an unconscious man's dick in my hand.

I look back at the doorway, expecting to see Sam standing there, but he's walled himself up in our bedroom. He's sick of me today, and that's fine. I'll find other ways to occupy my time.

I crawl across the floor, grab the plastic wolf mask, and bring it over to him. Fisting his hair, I raise his head and straddle his lap to slip the mask over his face. He looks so malevolent behind the plastic. So different, like he's a part of something I desperately need to know about.

Warmth radiates from his lap to my bare thighs with a stoney heat that caresses my skin in a way I haven't felt in a long time. I throb with an ache I haven't felt in even longer. Maybe since I was a teenager watching movies I shouldn't have watched. I wanted that passion. That feral draw to another person. But I ended up with Sam, who loves to remind me that he was there to shove my broken pieces together.

I sit on my heels, lowering myself on his lap and resting my pussy on his cock, the thin panties the only thing between us. Heat radiates from his skin. I tilt my hips, lifting my pelvis and dragging myself along the length of his dick. I rub over the ridges the bars make beneath the thin skin.

Holy hell. The pleasure immediately hits differently than when fingers or hands prod me. Even a tongue feels different from this. I draw my hips back, raking my clit against his dick through my panties. This dude is fucking ribbed for *my* pleasure.

"Oh god," I whisper, gripping his shoulders. This action is so raw and immature, yet it sends electricity coursing through my body.

I ride his length, dry-humping him until I soak his skin through my panties. I play with the tempo and pressure until my eyes roll into the back of my head as I chase my pleasure.

Mine and only mine.

I grip the sides of his mask, pressing my forehead against the plastic barrier shielding me from evil. My fingers dig into it, crinkling it a bit as I feel my approaching orgasm barrel down on me.

I bite my lip as hard as I can to keep the sounds from escaping. Pleasure takes me in a chokehold and doesn't release me until I feel like I might faint. My hips jerk, and I nearly split the mask in two as I scream in my head.

When I'm finished, I climb off him and put my hand over my mouth. The heavy weight of guilt crushes me until I can't breathe. Even though I didn't kiss him or do anything but take advantage of what was lying beneath me, I'm pretty sure I just cheated on Sam.

Knox's mask stares back at me as his head leans against the wall. No one can know I came on his dick. I can't ever—

His eyes open and seek out mine.

Oh god. What does he remember? Was he aware of what I did to him? If he knows, I can't keep him alive.

CHAPTER 11

KNOX

"Where am I?" I whisper, and the girl takes a relieved breath.

I won't let on that I felt everything she did to me because I was awake the entire time. She's stupid if she thinks I'd drink something she offered. Most of whatever was in that cup has been absorbed by the floor.

Her touch on my dick, though? Oh god. Then she climbed onto my lap and rode me like I've never felt before. I had to play dumb. With the way her hand was clamped over her mouth, I don't think she intended to come while using me. I don't know. But I fucking loved it, and I'm aching for her warm, slick, panty-covered pussy grinding on my bare skin.

Then she picks up a fucking hammer, and my cock recedes inside me. Instead of calming her, the orgasm seems to have left her angrier.

"Good morning," she says, tapping the head of the hammer on her upturned palm.

I look at the morning glow pouring through the bedroom window. A dim blue stares back at me instead of the blackness

I expected. My eyes search for a clock, and when I find one, I tug at the chains. It's after six in the morning. She has no idea what she's sentencing me to if she doesn't let me get to that party.

"I have to go," I say, raising my eyes to hers. I realize I'm wearing my mask again, and I reach up to take it off.

"Leave it on for this."

"For what?"

"Tell me who they are," she says.

Is she going to bludgeon me with that hammer if I don't? After coming on my lap? That's extra fucked up.

"I . . . can't," I say. She doesn't understand. I literally fucking can't.

She drops to her knees, and before I can react, she slams a nail through my sack and hits it with the head of the hammer. She literally just played pin the tail on the donkey with my scrotum. I scream out as a blinding pain races from my nuts to my dick, and then the rest of my body floods with a sharp heat. I have *never* felt such a burning feeling.

I instinctively go to draw my legs up, but I'm nailed to the floor. Any movement sends another bolt of pain through me. I force my legs down, thankful she didn't hit my balls with the hammer as well. I don't think she did, at least.

But then she comes at me with another nail, and all grateful feelings dissolve.

"I thought you'd be okay with another piercing," she says as she slides a finger over one of the metal barbells in my dick.

"This is not how I expected this date to go," I say. Spit gathers and comes out of my mouth with every pained word.

"So you were awake for that?"

"Of course I was awake, you sadistic bitch! Who gets off and goes right to violence like this?"

"Karma, I guess."

"Karma's a cunt," I say.

I probably deserve this. My hand has held knives and guns that killed others. My bare hands have taken lives. I've done everything treacherous to belong right here, with her come on my dick and metal nails in my ball sack. I probably deserve one right through my cock, but let's not give her ideas.

My nut skin tenses as I try to switch my weight to my other hip.

"Are you going to tell me yet? Or do I need to send a nail through your hands like your people did to my father?"

"Is that what this is about? A decade-long vendetta?"

"Losing a parent in such a traumatic way makes it a little easier to hold on to a grudge for that long," she snaps.

"I didn't hurt you or your father," I remind her.

"You're all I have connecting me to whoever did."

"And you think nailing my balls to the floor will somehow make up for your father's death?"

She tightens her lips. "I don't know how else to get you to talk."

"Have you considered being fucking nice?"

She laughs. "I don't think that will work with someone like you."

"You're right. But grind on my dick some more, and I just might spill my guts."

"That's not happening again," she says with a glare.

It'll happen about three hundred more times in my head, I'll tell you that. Even though she's crazy, the girl can move her hips, and I'm just about willing to give up everyone for a chance to be inside her. Even nailed to the fucking floor, I bet I could still get hard if she asked me to.

Am I simping for a woman with a hammer and all the balls to nail mine to the floor? Absolutely.

Her boyfriend shows up in the doorway, and a dark laugh leaves him. I'm dripping in sweat from the pain at this point, and if anyone would understand, it's him.

"Baby, you didn't," he says.

He pulls the hammer from her hand and uses the back to pull out the nail heads. I don't know what hurts worse, the going in or the coming out, but my soul leaves my body as he removes them. They land on the floor beside me, rolling idly and covered in my blood. He smirks at me.

"I don't know if I should be afraid," he says.

Based on that bruise on her face and the old one on her shoulder, he probably should be. A man who lays a hand on a woman deserves more than nails driven into his balls.

"I would be," I say, and his face tightens into a grimace.

As he pulls my mask away from my face, he doesn't seem to recognize me. He must be a new kind of stupid. He throws my shirt at me, and I use it to stem the bleeding, which isn't bleeding the way I thought it would. This is turning into the worst Reckoning I could have imagined.

Somehow, even worse than the last.

CHAPTER 12

ALLISTER

Sam let Knox off the chain to go to the bathroom and clean up. I said to let him rot. Either way, he's back on his chain now. I hand a cup of water to him, and he drinks it down in a few gulps.

"Sam, would you be a peach and grab his other arm for me?" I ask.

Sam gives me a smirk as I rifle through the drawer. I pull out an archaic-looking device I had Sam make. It's a modified shock collar, but it's not meant for his neck.

"What? No!" Knox says, fighting Sam over his right arm's freedom.

I lean over his legs and steady them as he flails and fights me. He yells out, as if anyone can hear him. We're in the middle of nowhere. He can scream until his voice breaks.

I work the ring over his flaccid cock and push it to the base. I hope it hurts. I had anticipated catching a man, and what better way to make a man talk than to shock the shit out of his dick? I wasn't going to use it on him, but then I realized he faked sleeping while I rode him. I fully intend to get him back for that while I try to coax information out of him.

I lock the device and set the key on the dresser, very far from him. Sam leaves me alone with him again. He isn't into these interrogations. Maybe he can't handle what I plan to do with Knox's genitals.

"What is this thing?" he asks, trying to tug on it with his free hand. It doesn't come off, even as his tugging grows more desperate. "What the fuck is this?"

"It's a shock ring," I tell him with a smile.

"You wouldn't."

I grab the remote and turn it on, and a soft hum fills the room as I power it all the way up. "If you get hard, I absolutely will. Unless, of course, you end this all right now and give up who they are."

"I won't get hard with this thing on me," he says with a certainty that's almost laughable.

"We'll see about that," I say.

Soon, he'll have no choice. We cut the water to the bathroom so he couldn't drink from there when he cleaned up with the damp rag we offered him. After going so long without water, he happily drank down what I handed him, which also contained two dissolved pills in a very particular shade of blue. When it comes to getting hard, he won't have a choice in the matter.

I hope it hurts. I hope it's so fucking uncomfortable. And I love that he'll get no release. Again.

I sit on the bed beside my little stuffed rabbit until I hear the sound of the ring coming to life. He screams out in agony and clutches his dick.

"Goddamn it, what did you give me?" he asks, but he has to know.

I hit the manual override and depress the button. "Care to tell me who you work for before I turn this thing back on?"

"Over my dead body."

"Why do I feel like that's what this will come to?"

"It won't make you feel better, you know," he says. "You already killed one of us, and you don't feel any different, do you? The scales haven't tilted back in your favor, even after you nailed my balls to the floor."

His words bite a little. I do worry I won't feel different when I kill him, but I can't let him leave now. He's seen too much. He knows too much. And I know nothing at all.

"How frustrating would it be to get hard and have someone pleasing themself in front of you?" I ask. "Someone you can't touch as you anticipate every upcoming shock?"

I reach back and untie the strap around my neck. The fabric falls, exposing my breasts. I smirk at him as he reaches over and puts his mask back on. He's concealing some of me, I guess, so I move forward and drop to my knees in front of him before falling backward on my ass. I spread my thighs for him. Black panties cover most of my pussy, but a shadow of what he wants peeks from beneath.

He lets out a breath.

"How frustrated are you right now?" I ask as I slide my fingers back and slip them inside me.

Knox clutches his dick. "Painfully."

"I bet you wish you could come, huh?"

He raises his mask and gives me the most fucked-up smirk I've ever seen. "It's cute that you think I won't come to you. Even through the shocks. As if I haven't been thinking about you on my dick every moment since you got off it."

The deep, gravelly sexuality oozing from every word takes me off guard, so I do the only thing I can think of doing. I release the button, and a shock goes through him again.

His ass lifts off the floor, and he leans over, trying to catch his breath. The shocks are time sensitive once engaged. Every minute he's erect, he'll get shocked.

He flips his mask down and squares up on the ground again. His hand strokes the head of his cock as he watches me. He matches my speed as I fuck myself with my fingers. The faster I go, the harder he goes. A minute passes, and a shock courses through him again. As he curls up against the pain, he doesn't stop stroking himself. I bring my fingers to my mouth and suck on my wetness. He groans when I do. Not from pain, but from pleasure.

"You're so fucked up," he grits out.

"Says the one jerking off through copious amounts of electricity."

Why am I so turned on by this? God. This man is so attracted to me that he's literally fighting electrical forces to get off to me. Maybe he's just stubborn enough to prove a point, but either way, I fucking like it. Bull-headed meets bull-headed.

"Get on my lap again, karma, and let me show you how I can come no matter what you're doing to me."

Another round of electricity goes through him, and the muscles in his groin contract and spasm as he keeps stroking his dick.

But why am I even considering his offer? No. I can't let him fuck me. Even if he gave me all the information I asked for, I'm with Sam. The moment I say his name in my head, the bruises tingle around my eye and on my shoulder, almost scolding me.

I stand up and position myself above the footboard, straddling it. He brings his chained hand upward. A ring of discoloration marks his wrist, but he seizes the opportunity to slip his fingers through my wetness. I lower myself on two of his fingers, taking them inside me. He moans as I lift and lower myself on his hand, riding it like I would his cock. I hold myself up by gripping the metal beneath me as my thighs begin to tremble.

"Why won't you let me fuck you?" he pants.

"Just shut up and let me ride your hand."

"So I can't fuck karma, but she can fuck me?" he asks.

"Be grateful you get to feel me with your fingers."

He groans, and I feel bad for even allowing this, but using him for my selfish pleasure doesn't change my overall plan for him.

Another shock rips through his dick. His strokes slow, and beads of white shoot from his cock and slip down his hand and shaft. Another shock goes through him, and I come too. I shove my hand over my mouth to hide my moans as I lose control of myself. Liquid gushes down his arm and saturates the floor.

My chest rises and falls as I try to catch my breath. I reach over and hit the manual override button again. He just stays inside me, come dripping from us both. He anticipates the next shock, only to realize it's not coming.

In my orgasm-induced state of calm, I don't realize he's climbing up to his knees, raising his mask, and reaching for my hair. He grabs beneath my bun and drags me close to his face. This is his chance to kill me if he really wants to, with his other hand still buried inside me.

Instead, he kisses me, pouring all his pain into my mouth.

"Better watch yourself, pretty girl, because the moment I'm off this chain, I'll get inside you."

"*If* you get off your chain."

My words drip with confidence, and I have no desire to release him, but that smirk he offers shakes something loose inside me. It's like he knows a secret I don't. Well, I'm sick and tired of secrets. I'll figure out a way to make him talk, and once he tells me everything I need to know, I'll be done with him. That's if I can stop using him as a sex toy.

Maybe I could take him with me . . .

Sam doesn't know it yet, but we're through. I've already

packed a bag and tucked it under the couch. As soon as this night from hell is over, I'm getting the fuck out of this godforsaken town and never looking back. But there's always the risk that Sam could come after me. Maybe keeping this guy around as a personal attack dog isn't such a bad idea.

Before any of that, though, I need to know who killed my father, and I need to make them pay. If I have to kill everyone in front of me to get answers, so be it. Karma is coming, and she's not taking anyone's shit anymore.

CHAPTER 13

KNOX

The queen of darkness lets me put on my pants. How nice of her. Maybe she's done torturing my cock and balls. I sit with my pants unzipped and unbuttoned, the fabric spread to expose the fine, dark hairs.

Speaking of the queen of darkness, where is she? She left pretty soon after my hand was inside her. I bring that hand up to my nose and smell the remnants of her sweet cunt on my fingers.

Who knew karma would smell so sinful?

I stare at the clock. It's pushing seven a.m. It's too late to get to the party now. Fuck me. She might as well kill me at this point. They'll do it if she doesn't, and I'd rather it happens at her fucked-up, pretty little hands.

I hear noises outside the closed door. Harsh whispers rise to a discernable sound, and I realize it's her voice saying, *"Absolutely not. You can't do that."*

What can't he do?

And then I hear a smack.

She shrieks, and I lean against the chain.

Here's the thing, I don't think I deserve much of anything in the world, but I could deserve her. If nothing else, I can treat her better than her current choice of man. Even with a couple holes in my nut sack, I still never thought to hit her, though she probably fucking deserved it in that moment.

The door whips open and her boyfriend carries a box into the room. What now? What new torture device has she come up with for me? Not that it matters. I'd probably give up the Exodus at this point because I'm going to die anyway.

But I won't give any information to *him*. Only her.

Karma skulks out from behind him, her hand on her right cheek. She drops it and raises her chin stoically, despite the red flush of his handprint on her face. I don't need his name on a list to want to kill him.

"Who do you work for?" his deep voice asks as he sets the box on the ground.

"Fuck. Off," I say.

"I thought you'd say that." He lifts the lid off the box, and two big black ears rise over the cardboard edge.

He didn't.

"When I found out you had a son, I thought he'd be a great bargaining chip. But then I found this."

He picks up Petey, and the rabbit takes a gnarly chunk out of his hand. He bites everyone but me.

"Fucker," Sam hisses as he throws my rabbit back into the box. He shoves the lid in place and turns his rabid eyes toward me as he draws a knife from his belt. He holds the blade down, twisting the sharp tip on the box lid. "Who do you fucking work for?" Blood drips from the wound in his hand and rolls down the knife handle.

He wouldn't.

"Don't!" the girl says, eyes wide.

She rushes toward the box to pull it out from under his blade, but he grips her arm to stop her. He puts the knife between his teeth and punches her in the face. Her body slides across the floor and lands with a bang against the dresser. The lamp leaps from the table and shatters at her feet.

I crawl to the very end of my chain and lean toward her.

Not my karma.

Before I can turn back toward the walking-talking piece of flaming-hot shit, I hear the sound of the blade slicing through cardboard. I close my eyes, almost too afraid to look, but I force myself. I turn and see the handle, so I reach for it, straining to catch a corner of the cardboard.

Not my fucking rabbit.

"You fucker!" I yell, straining against the metal holding me back. This is worse than everything else they've done to me. None of that mattered. What matters is that rabbit and that girl.

I hear a squeal as the metal pole strains against my weight and rage. Say what you will about the Exodus, but they made me into this feral animal on a chain. The sheer strength and willpower they forced out of me strains the metal's integrity until it gives, breaking off from the base and throwing me forward onto my hands and knees.

My eyes focus on him. I swing the pole and catch it, pulling my hand free. I draw my arm back and bring the pole across me like a bat, connecting the stout metal with his head. He flies to the side and lands on the ground.

"That's for her," I grit out, and she screams.

Why does she scream? I don't fucking know. Is she upset with what I've done, or is she now seeing me as a personification of her childhood nightmares? Am I the monster that just crawled out of her closet?

I take a moment to help her to her feet, and she just stares at me like she isn't sure if she needs to defend herself against me too. She doesn't. I won't harm her. Instead, I walk to her shit-stain boyfriend lying on the ground. He looks up at me, begging me, I think, but I hear only the hammering of my heartbeat in my ears. I stab the hollow end of the pole through his abdomen, sinking it deep enough to hit the floor on the other side.

"And that's for my rabbit!"

Blood rises and spurts out of his mouth, blending with the crimson coating his face. His head is split open, a shiny glimpse of his white skull showing beneath his blood-soaked hair. If that wasn't going to kill him, the stabbing sure will.

I turn my attention to the box. I don't hear any sound coming from it, no claws on cardboard or gentle snuffles. It's a silent, ominous rectangle sitting in front of me on the floor. I almost can't bring myself to check. If I open it up and see that my baby is dead, I don't think I can leave this house standing. I will burn us all down inside it.

I would burn the world down for that fucking rabbit.

I drop to my knees and lean over the box. I say a prayer to anyone who will listen. If it's the devil, so be it. I'll owe him one if Petey's okay. I'll do his fucking dirty work for him if it means I can hug my boy again.

With shaking hands, I lift the lid away, and my eyes immediately go to the knife blade. Blood covers the metal. My heart sinks as all my training and conditioning goes out the window. But then I see those two big ears twitch toward me, and my heart beats again.

"Petey!" I say, lifting him from the box.

There's a wet spot on his fur, and as my fingers wipe through it, I realize it's blood. I set him in my lap and spread the dense fur, but I see no injury. He wasn't hit. All the blood must have been from that piece of shit's bite wound—which he fucking deserved.

"You're crying," the girl says as she drops in front of me and hands my shirt to me.

I wipe the rogue tears from my cheeks. "I'm not crying. It's just a rabbit."

That crazy conditioning rears up and reminds me to be tough. Be hard. Be cold.

"It's not just a rabbit." Her eyes rise to mine. "He's your son."

I look down at his big, dark eyes. The whites have receded, and the fear leaves him as if it never happened. I wish things worked the same for me.

He wants off my lap, feeling the urge to go explore the room as he would in our own home, but there are nails and shit somewhere, so I don't let him. The room needs to be rabbit proofed before I'll let him wander around. I stick him back in the box, rip the knife from the lid, and set the lid back on top.

I stand up, and she mirrors my movements. She reaches out and grabs my arm. I pivot, pushing her against the wall as my hand rises to her throat, the chain still dangling from my other arm.

"Tell me your name, karma."

Her wide eyes go white with fear. She swallows, and her throat moves beneath my hand.

"Allister," she whispers over my grip. "Why did you kill him for me? After what I've done to you?"

I push the hair away from her face and brush her cheek, then continue downward until I reach her mouth. I ease my fingers past her lips. "Remember what I said? The moment I got off this chain, I said I'd be inside you. I don't make promises I can't keep."

My knee juts between her legs and spreads her thighs. The hard head of my cock peeks from beneath the black fabric, still unzipped and unbuttoned. I pull it downward, freeing it.

Fuck the pain in my balls. Nothing can keep me from her now.

I tug her panties aside and lift her thigh. I lean in and kiss her, hard and fast, like I need her lips to survive the next hour. The next minute. Maybe the next second. I devour her chest as I nip at her flesh. I would have fucked her whether her boyfriend was dead or alive, but she seems to only be welcoming my touch with his dead body beside us.

Then the warm sting of metal presses against my throat.

I release her, and a devilish smirk crosses her face. Clearly, she hasn't forgiven me like I'd hoped. I should be the one who needs to be coerced to forgive *her*! She's the one who nailed my balls to the floor.

I lift my hands, and she backs me up until I tumble onto the bed. Scratchy cotton sheets nip at my bare back. She climbs over me, the knife still at my throat. Any normal person would look for ways to unarm their assailant, but I just keep my eyes on hers as she threatens to kill me.

She raises her skirt and cuts off her panties. That was my moment to escape, with the blade so far from my neck, but not even the imminent threat of death could take me from the promise buried within that motion. She puts the steel back to my throat, and I throb at the heat of her over me. On me. Soaking me.

"Tell me who you work for," she says, putting weight into the blade.

"After I fuck you."

I draw my hips back, tracing her slit until I know I'm right against her entrance. I push my hips upward, and her pussy envelops me. She wraps around me so fucking tightly that I release a raspy groan. It's as if all her hatred for me is squeezing and strangling my dick.

There's a flicker of pleasure on her face before she becomes as steely as the blade at my neck.

"I should kill you," she says, moving herself on my lap. She rises and comes down on me, using me and selfishly rocking her hips. My piercings disappear inside her.

"Cut my throat, karma. Bathe yourself in my blood as you fuck yourself with my cock."

Did I just say that? Absolutely. Did I mean it? Without a doubt.

She leans back, taking the knife from my throat and putting it between her legs, right against my hard flesh.

"What if I sever your dick while it's still inside me?"

"You're crazy, but you're not dumb, baby. You want the blood right where it is, filling my cock so I can keep you stuffed."

"Don't call me crazy," she says, still moving on my lap. She cuts into me, and I bite my lip to keep from screaming out. Warm blood trickles down and nestles in the pool of my pelvis.

Why does this girl insist on mutilating my genitals? And why doesn't it make my dick recede into my body in fear for its life?

I guess we're both a little crazy.

Allister eases down my length, putting pressure on the cut with the walls of her pussy. She uses my blood as lubricant, and no amount of pain could keep me from enjoying that sight. Each downward movement gathers more and more scarlet liquid until she's covered in it.

I roll her onto her back. Judging by the way she grits her teeth, she hates losing the control, and being beneath me is clearly beneath her.

"Listen to me," I say. "Hate me all you want, but don't let that keep you from coming on my dick. You don't have to like me to get the release you so desperately need."

"Fuck you!" she screams, and the tone wrestles with pleasure as I pin her arms above her head. The knife remains in her clenched fist.

My dick hurts. My balls ache. And yet I hammer her the way I know that fucker never has. A woman like her doesn't go feral if she's getting dicked-down the way she needs. It's also easy to forget the pain when she moans.

"Play with yourself," I say, releasing one of her hands.

She reaches over and grabs the knife, and I think this is it, that she's going to cut my throat and bathe in my blood, but she brings the blade to her mouth and runs her tongue up the shining edge. She clasps it between her teeth before dropping her hand to rub herself. She's so wet and bloody.

Who knew karma could be so unhinged?

She tightens on me as she rubs quick circles around her clit. Her lips spread, and she whimpers, exposing red-tinged teeth still clamped on the knife. It almost feels like a test. As if she's wondering if I'll take the opportunity to turn the tables and put that blade against her pretty throat.

She comes around me, her back arching beautifully as her chest lifts into mine. I grab the knife from her, wrapping my hand around the handle as I tug it from her mouth. The look of fear momentarily blips across her face, but she relaxes as I run the blade across her breasts.

Then I look karma dead in the eyes as I fuck and fill her.

I stay in her for a moment, savoring the feeling of her before I pull out. We're a bloody mess, and yet I drag the blade down her body until it lands between her legs. I stuff the handle inside her, and red-tinged come rises up as I fuck her with it until she's screaming.

"Knox," she says on the next moan.

I bury my face between her legs. The tip of the knife rakes against my shoulder as I devour her bloody, come-coated clit. The salty, metallic taste assaults my tongue, but I can think of nothing more I want to fill my belly with. I eat her while thrusting the knife in and out of her until she's dripping all the remnants of our pleasure onto the floor.

My tongue curls around her clit before flicking and sucking on her. Her moans rise and intensify, growing with every thrust of the knife and lash of my tongue.

"Come again, karma. Coat my chin, and I'll tell you everything you want to know."

CHAPTER 14

ALLISTER

Steam follows me out of the bathroom after my shower. When I walk into the bedroom, Knox has his giant rabbit draped across his lap. I never thought I'd find such a thing sexy, but here we are. His messy hair shakes as he leans over to worship that creature. I can't tell what he's saying, but it's clearly full of the sort of love I haven't felt in a long time.

"He tried to eat your boyfriend," he says, so nonchalantly.

My eyes drop to the bloody mound that hardly bears a resemblance to Sam any longer. The rabbit chewed a hole through his pant leg.

"What do I do with him?" I ask.

"Typically, they take care of cleanup for me."

"Who's they?"

He promised he'd tell me anything I want to know, and he better not go back on that. But men say all types of things when they're blind with lust. It doesn't mean they'll stick to it when the fog clears.

"It's an organization that runs this town," he says. "Maybe even the state. Massively powerful men and women."

I figured as much, and Sam fully believed that from the start.

"What do they call themselves?" I ask, but he shakes his head. "Don't make me get it out of you."

He eases the rabbit off his lap, and the animal hops down and thumps his massive feet on the hardwood floor before scurrying off.

"Get on your knees and let me shove my dick so far in your throat that you feel it in your gut. Then I'll tell you."

He stands up and wraps his hand in my hair as he drags me toward the bed and sits down. Blood paints the sheets, but he isn't fazed. He flicks open his slacks and takes out his cock.

"If you put that in my mouth, I'll bite it off," I say, my eyes narrowing.

"You won't do that. You're desperate for the name of your father's killer. Desperate enough to take me into your mouth."

I crane my neck like I'm going to suck him off, but I bite down on the head instead.

"You really have a vendetta against my dick, don't you?" he hisses through gritted teeth. "Let go!" he screams as I twist. "Exodus! They're called the Exodus! Now get your fucking teeth off my dick."

I release him, and he rips his hips backward, freeing his dick from my mouth.

"What the hell's the matter with you?" he growls, rubbing his hand over the head of his dick. "I have so many other things for you to latch on to, but no, you have to go for my junk. Again."

I wipe my lips. "I think men are more receptive to interrogation when their manhood is at risk."

"If you had kidnapped anyone else, they'd kill you for what you've done."

"But you?"

"I like them a bit unhinged."

I crawl up his body and knock his head onto the bed by grasping his hair. I straddle his face.

"Then be a good boy and make me even crazier." I hover over his mouth as his hands hook around my thighs.

"If you're going to demand something like this, sit on my fucking face. I want to suffocate beneath you while you come."

He grips my thighs and pulls me down, and then I lower my weight into my heels and drop onto his face. His tongue and lips work everything beneath me. I moan as we wrestle for some semblance of control or power. He snatches it away from me before giving it right back.

I ride his face, up and down, back and forth, until I'm skating toward another orgasm. I toy with him, leaning off his mouth so he can take several deep breaths before I suffocate him with my weight. And he lets me.

He shakes his head beneath me like a ravenous animal trying to eat his way out. My eyes roll to the back of my head as his tightening grip—a sign that he's struggling for that next breath—brings me closer.

He taps my thigh and I lift off his mouth. This is the kind of breath play I could get used to.

"You still aren't sitting hard enough. Sit on my fucking face. Soak my mouth, karma. Come all over my chin."

The moment the last syllable leaves his lips, I drop my weight again. I sit deep, feeling the warmth of his nose, tongue, lips, and breath everywhere between my legs. I ride his face harder. He grips my thighs, and I don't let up. He wants me to really sit, so I'm really fucking sitting. I'll let him die beneath me if that's what it takes. I'm going to get mine.

And I do. I come, hard, with his chest surging beneath me for a breath that I refuse to give him. I put my orgasm above his most basic necessity.

I'm an asshole.

I sit up on my knees, and he gasps for air. His mouth and chin glisten with my come.

"My turn," he says as he rolls me off him.

"I'm not sucking your dick," I remind him.

"Your mouth isn't where I want to put my cock."

He climbs off the bed and grabs his mask. He wipes his face on the back of his arm before slipping the plastic over his face. Chills wash across me. There's a fear I didn't expect as he dons that mask. It was different when he was chained up. Now he's free and can be as dangerous as he desires.

I sit up, curling my legs beneath me as I lean over the bed. "Get down on the ground and crawl to me."

"Really?" he asks with a hesitant shake of his head.

"If you want to get inside me, dog, you'll get on the floor and crawl to me."

He blinks at me through the holes in the mask, and I'm not sure he'll do as I asked. Then his knees come out from beneath him, and he lands on them. His hands drop to the floor, and he moves each limb individually as he fucking crawls to me. Hand over hand. Knee over knee.

A low growl vibrates off the mask as he ends up beneath me, his eyes rising to mine as he gets to his feet and wraps his fingers around my throat. His hands roughly spread my legs, and when I reach for the mask, he pins both my wrists above my head. The power dynamic has shifted again, and that familiar fear returns as he crawls over me, putting my back to the mattress.

"Face your fears, karma. The man behind this mask is a monstrosity, but he's not your monster."

He pushes inside me, and a groan follows my frustrated exhale. He looks like a monster, and I don't like losing my power to a wild animal cloaked in human skin as he takes what he wants. But he's also giving me what I want. What I need.

It's been so long since I felt such carnal pleasures without harsh words for pillow talk.

So I lean into my fear, wrapping him up in my legs and pulling him closer to me. His hips grind on mine, and I feel so fucking helpless to his onslaught.

"Fuck!" I scream. For some fucked-up reason, this man does something otherworldly to me and my body. Especially those fucking piercings. I've *never* felt such a thing.

His thrusts slow, as if he's trying to hold out. "You feel so fucking good," he whispers.

I take in the features of his mask before I close my eyes and bask in the movement of his hips. I want to rip the plastic off and make him kiss me, but I'm pinned and helpless beneath him. I've been forced to hand my power to him, and I hate to say that I like the familiarity.

"I'm going to come, karma," he groans, and his hips stutter against mine.

I'm helpless to stop the monster from filling me. But who's more of the monster? The one between my legs or the man I've been living with all along?

Not all masks are plastic.

CHAPTER 15

KNOX

I sent Allister to the hardware store for lime while I moved Sam's body outside. I've never had to clean up a body because the Exodus has always taken care of it, but I've seen them dissolve the bodies until they were unrecognizable, so that's what I'm going to try. The lime doesn't dissolve anything, but it will keep the smell down and the scavengers away while Mother Nature does her thing.

I also tasked Allister with picking up a cat litter box and rabbit food for Petey because I can almost guarantee the Exodus members are waiting for me at my apartment. I told her not to go near that place again. Her little game of captivity put me on their radar. I'm now considered their enemy.

I bring the body as far into the woods behind their house as I can, then start digging a grave. Allister shows up a while later, with two bags of lime in each of her hands. I grab them from her and kick his body into the grave before covering him with lime and soil.

When I look back and see her staring at the hole, I feel a moment of guilt. She looks almost . . . sad. Unfortunately, he sealed his fate the moment I saw him hit her. His threat to my boy just brought swifter justice.

She keeps her eyes locked on the covered grave. "Do you think his spirit will find out I came on your dick before he even died?"

"He's dead, and you're worried about a little infidelity?"

"I don't know. I wish I felt worse about everything."

"Well, he treated you like shit." I step into her and rub my thumb along the bruises on her face. "He deserved death the first time he put one of these on you."

"High moral ground for a killer," she clips, and a smirk crosses her face.

"Oh, sweetheart, I showed you I had no values when I fucked and ate you in the same room as his dead body." I bring my lips close to hers. "And because you nearly drowned me with your come, I question *your* values."

She blows out a breath that carries some embarrassment.

Despite what she's done to me, and despite the hatred in her body, I can't deny my attraction to her. It's not just physical, even though she's perfect. It's her personality. She's so powerful, yet she's only just realizing how much power she can hold over a man.

The way she raises her chin when she speaks to me, as if I'm less than her. The way she uses my body for her pleasure. She drives me wild.

I lift her chin, the rare moment it's down. "You have beautifully fucked-up values, karma."

Her eyelids flutter as if she's fighting back tears. "I've lost so much in search of the truth. Trying to find my father's killer. I even lost myself in search of revenge."

"I think you've found yourself, Allister." I wipe her hair away from her sweaty face. "Did your father say anything when you found him?"

Her eyes race from left to right as she digs into her

memory. There's no way her father's killer said his real name, but maybe he gave some kind of hint that will help me sniff out his identity.

"He said something about a golden giraffe."

Golden giraffe. There's an elder who wears a giraffe mask. It's the only one I've ever seen, and it stands out because it's such an odd choice of animal.

It has to be Mark.

"Let me think about this," I say.

"If you can't tell me a name yet, at least tell me why they do this."

"I wish I could tell you it was anything more than their rich boredom. An exercise of power."

Her lower lip trembles. "My father was killed because some rich assholes were bored?"

"I was almost killed because of it too."

"Is that why you joined them? Because it was that or be killed?"

"Sometimes monsters aren't born but made that way."

"Tell me what happened to you. I want to know everything."

So I do. I detail how Adam captured me and dragged me to the party before giving me an impossible ultimatum: kill or be killed. I even explain how they trained me for over a year, keeping me locked away until they were sure I'd been broken.

"Clearly, they didn't fully break you," she says. "You killed your handler."

I shrug my shoulders. "Even the most obedient dog will turn on you if you kick it hard enough."

Adam has been kicking me for years. I'm only surprised it took me this long to snap. Then I look at Allister, and I realize the actual catalyst. If her virtue hadn't been in danger, would I have attacked Adam?

Probably not.

"Well, now you have all the answers, so I guess it's time to tie off the last loose end," I say. "Can you at least promise you'll take care of Petey when I'm gone?"

She shakes her head. "I haven't decided your fate yet, and I definitely don't have all the answers. I want the guy with the giraffe mask."

"You fail to realize how difficult it'll be for me to help you further. By keeping me out past the party, I've been labeled as a deserter. They'll be looking for me now."

Her gaze falls to the grass as she realizes she's reached a dead end. "So all of this . . . was for nothing? I can't avenge my father's death. Is that what you're trying to tell me?"

When she looks at me again, my heart breaks. Tears fill her eyes, and her chin positioning lacks its usual height. I wish I could give her what she needs, but I can't. That would be like going into the lion's den with a meat suit for protection. If she plans to kill me, so be it, but I won't give the Exodus the satisfaction.

CHAPTER 16

ALLISTER

"I need your car," Knox says as he walks into my bedroom.

"What, no!" I sit up taller.

"What? Do you think I won't come back?" he says.

I shake my head, but that's exactly what I think. If I were him, I'd leave and never look back. I nailed his nut sack to the floor, for fuck's sake, and now he can't go home. I'm stuck with him and Sam's ghost because of my rabid need for vengeance.

Knox swivels his head, looking around the room for something. His eyes land on the rabbit, and he scoops Petey into his arms. He walks over and plops the massive rabbit onto my lap. I stroke his fur and rub his cheek.

Knox cocks his head and studies us. "Weird. He usually bites everyone but me."

My hands move away from the rabbit's face. "You put a giant-ass rabbit on my lap who routinely fucking bites?"

"He seems to like you. Or maybe he knows you'll bite back," he says with a smirk. "Anyway, I won't go anywhere without him, so can I please borrow your car?"

He makes a really good point. He adores this rabbit, and as long as I hold on to him, he's guaranteed to return.

"Fine." I lean over, straining beneath the weight of this dog-sized rabbit, and grab my key off the nightstand.

Knox leaves, and I drop my hand to Petey's back. I've never seen such a rugged man with a rabbit as a pet. I could see a man like him eating one of these, not cuddling it. Killing it instead of killing for it.

For him *and*—

Well, me.

It's comforting to run my hand through his thick, soft coat. I've never wanted kids, nor did I want to bring one into the fucked-up little relationship I shared with Sam. Even so, I felt an urge to take care of something, so I brought a kitten home once. Sam told me I couldn't have a pet, and then he took the kitten and left with it. I never saw it again. Not wanting that fate to befall another animal, I didn't bring anything home after that.

I idly pet Petey, thinking about how lost I suddenly feel. The drive for revenge has fueled my entire adult life, though I'll likely never know who killed my father. Or have any way to avenge his death. It feels like my efforts have all been for nothing.

The worst part is that the only silver lining in this is that Sam is dead and I'm free from his control and abuse. My freedom is now in my hands, and I'm choosing to use it very unwisely by shacking up with someone from the infamous group that murdered my dad. Letting Knox live means letting my father's vengeance die.

I considered telling him to take my car and the rabbit and get the hell out of here. Part of me worries he'll kill me and dump my body somewhere after everything I did to him, but something about the way he gingerly placed this rabbit into my lap made me certain he was coming back. For both of us.

I lift Petey and look into his eyes. "I'd have to compete with you if I dated your dad, huh?"

His nose twitches.

Yeah, I would.

"You probably should bite me. I did terrible things to your father."

I'm not sure how much time passes as I sit with Petey, but the rumble of tires eventually grates over the gravel driveway. Considering I kidnapped a man who buried my dead boyfriend in the backyard, I can't be certain if it's the police or the man I kidnapped. I peek through the blinds and heave a sigh of relief when I see my red sedan parked in the driveway.

I can't see the front of the vehicle. After straining for a moment, I back away and sit on the couch. I think of Sam in this room, pulling me onto his lap and squeezing a bruise he left on my thigh. His shouts echo between my ears—a reminder of all the ways I was never good enough.

The sound of the front door silences the intrusive memories. I take a breath, trying to slow my racing heart. I don't want to look weak. I don't want to *be* weak anymore.

I stand up and walk toward him as he enters the doorway to the living room, but he pushes his palm toward me, telling me to stop. He's covered in sweat, his entire form taking up the doorway, and he's straining to hold something off to the side, just behind the wall where I can't see it.

"Knox, what is this?" I ask.

Before I can step closer, he pushes a man toward me. The man's arms are bound behind his back with tape, but when Knox spins him around, I gasp. He's wearing a gold mask.

A gold *giraffe* mask.

I'm frozen in place when I see it staring back at me, the subject of my vengeance finally in front of me. He's not an adjacent person like Knox. He's the epicenter of my childhood nightmares. The man who is single-handedly responsible for ruining my life and dictating every shitty thing I've done since that fateful night.

Including dating Sam and kidnapping Knox.

"You—" I stare at the man before turning my attention back to Knox. "How?"

"Don't worry about how," he says, pulling his jacket closer to his side. "You deserve your karma."

The man tries to make a run for the door, but Knox draws his arm back and punches him in the face. The man stumbles backward and lands on the floor.

Even with Knox dangling my revenge in front of me, I bypass the man and rush to Knox's side. During the scuffle, I noticed a flash of red beneath his jacket. I lift the material away and see that his entire left side is covered in blood.

"It's nothing," he says, pushing my hand away from him. "I've been through much worse."

"Knox—"

"Karma is a bitch, remember? Go."

"Wait, what?"

"He's for you to kill."

Despite my rabid need for vengeance, I can't think of anything more than stopping Knox's bleeding, but he seems like he won't let me help him until I've gotten what he thinks I need. I'll have to compromise.

I walk over to the stranger's body and grip his ankles, then start dragging him toward the spare bedroom, past the dried blood stain. I lock him up, just as I did with Knox.

Knowing he can't go anywhere, I head back to the living room and find Knox on the couch. I stare at him. He smirks as his eyes rise to meet mine.

"Can my dying wish be to see you crawl across this floor to me?" he asks.

"You aren't going to die," I say.

"Crawl to me, karma," he whispers.

"If I crawl to you, will you let me tend to your injuries?"

"I'll consider it."

This fucking guy.

He lifts his shirt, showing fresh blood. I roll my eyes before dropping to my knees. If I have to play his game to save his life, so be it. I crawl toward him.

Our eyes remain locked on each other's, and I've never felt such a fucking compulsion to be in front of someone as I do right now. It's as if he's lassoed me and is slowly dragging me toward him. My knees rub on the rough wood, but I can't feel it. I can't feel anything but a warm draw to him.

"That's a good girl," he growls, and I melt into a puddle at his feet. I haven't felt like a good girl to anyone in a long time.

"Let me stop the bleeding, Knox," I say, biting my lip.

He winces as he lifts his hips and unzips his slacks. He pulls his cock from the fabric. "Why do I feel like the only way I'll get you to suck my dick is if you think I'll die if you don't?"

"You think highly of yourself," I clip.

He lifts his shirt again and puts his hand over the gash in his side. Blood spreads around his fingers. "I don't value myself too much if I'd die to have your mouth on me."

God, that hit me right between my legs. Sam wouldn't even run to the store for me when I was sick, and yet this man is lying here willing to bleed to death just to get a little of my attention.

And I think that warrants putting my lips around him.

I position myself between his legs. My gaze travels up his length before I lean forward and ease him into my mouth. I don't bite him this time. I just swirl my tongue around his head. He wraps his blood-coated hand in my hair, smearing crimson into the strands. He pushes me down on his cock and makes me choke on it.

The metal balls clack against my top teeth, and I try to widen my jaw to slip past them. He fucks himself, using his hand to control the depth and the speed. He uses me. And I allow it. And he doesn't seem to give a fuck if my teeth are raking his skin.

"Fuck," he groans, pulsing his hips against my face.

I release his dick and pull off my shirt. It's not for his pleasure, though I'm sure he likes the view of my bare tits in front of him. I put his dick in my mouth again, and he fucks my face. While he chokes me with his cock, I ball up my shirt and press it to his wound. I can't watch him bleed out any longer. I lean pressure into my hand as I suck him off until his thighs tremble around me and his hips stutter against my mouth.

I want to gain some control—I don't like feeling this out of it—so I take some back.

"Let me," I tell him, leaning up on my knees.

I put his cock between my breasts and wrap my free arm around my chest to pull them together. His cock glistens with my drool, disappearing and reappearing between the soft mounds of flesh.

"Karma," he whispers as he drops his head back.

"Come on my chest," I groan, feeling an uncomfortable ache between my legs at the sight between us. I fuck him until silky white beads shoot from him and coat my skin. When I release my breasts and sit up, the beads spread and drip down the curves of my nipples.

"You look fucking sexy with your tits covered in my come." Knox releases a satisfied exhale as his cock springs back against his bare abdomen. He strips off his shirt and uses it to wipe me clean. He leans forward and captures my mouth with his. "Good fucking girl."

I inwardly preen under his praise, but I'm careful to keep a look of indifference on my face. My body may react to him, but I have to be smart here. He's still one of them, and I still don't know if I can trust him.

CHAPTER 17

KNOX

Wet hair clings to my neck and forehead as bloody water travels down my body. Allister's shower head is so much better than mine, and I relax into the warmth as the water washes away the red.

I put my hand to the glued gash in my side. Mark fucking stabbed me. Allister wanted me to go to a hospital, but I absolutely can't. Exodus is deeply ingrained in this town. Probably this state. If I walk into a hospital, I won't be walking out. She finally caved and listened when I told her to use super glue. It's what I used for many of my injuries when I got my friendly initiation into the Exodus a decade ago.

I didn't die then, and I won't die this time, but I made sure Allister thought I would. It was the only way I could get her mouth on me. And besides, I actually could have died.

At least I'd have gone to hell with her perfect mouth and fantastic tits on my dick.

I drop my head back against the wall and let that image play in my mind like a beautiful fucking movie. Her full lips around my dick were heavenly, but what she did next was something beyond that. Celestial. She doesn't have big tits, but it didn't matter as she wrapped her arm around her body and squeezed them together so that her perfect, round mounds encased my cock.

I don't think I've had a woman please me in that way before, which makes me sound pathetic, but even fucking the backs of her fucking knees would have made me come like no other person I've ever been with.

Because it's her.

Thinking about my come dripping over her breasts and casting a glossy sheen over her nipples makes me want to get off again. I groan, wrapping my hand around my aching dick as my hand strokes past my piercings. I remember the way she looked covered in my pleasure, and it's all I need to send me over the edge.

I come against her shower wall, and it blends with the porcelain before washing away. I move my dick aside and examine my balls. The two holes have scabbed over now and, thankfully, she missed my actual testicles.

It doesn't make sense to obsess over someone who nailed my scrotum to the floor, but there's something about her. She's so strong, despite being battered down by someone else.

She reminds me of a circus animal—a lion, tiger, or elephant. Beasts that could rip a man apart if they wanted to, but they don't. They sit there, hold back their strength, and listen to the commands of some asshole. They take harsh whips and cruel words until they're forced to obey. But they never lose the power to kill. They're never tame. They're merely controlled.

Until they aren't.

A scream pierces the air and makes its way to the bathroom, and I can't help but wonder what terrible torture she's delivering to the man who changed her life so drastically. The man who made her kidnap and torture me.

I smile at the sound as it comes again. It's a beautiful melody that I hated to hear at my hands. But at her hands, even my own screams sound like a musical masterpiece.

Needing to bear witness to her song, I hurry out of the shower and dress.

CHAPTER 18

ALLISTER

His screams are music to my ears. They play over the screams of my father—the man this asshole tortured to death. My hammer comes down again and pushes a nail through his other hand. The nail head ends up flush with his skin as it locks him to the wall. He screams again, his mouth invisible behind that horrifying gold giraffe mask. One of the last things my father saw.

Besides me trying—and failing—to save him.

"Do you remember him?" I ask.

"Who?" the man screams, spit hurtling from his mouth.

"You nailed his hands, just like this." I slam the hammer against the nail one more time, pinching his muscle and flesh between drywall and metal.

"I didn't do shit!" he yells.

I turn, walk out of the room, and grab the picture of my father from the nightstand. When I'm back in the spare bedroom, I push the photo into his face. A photo of a time when my father was smiling and happy beside me. I was happy too. Before everything happened.

"Does he look familiar?" I ask.

"Fuck you!" he hisses. "And fuck you too, Knox."

I turn around and see Knox in the doorway. Heat creeps across my cheeks as he sees me in my worst form. My chest rises and falls as adrenaline dumps into my system, and I'm sure my eyes look absolutely crazed. I'm not sure why I have a moment of insecurity over my feral appearance. Knox has seen it. He's felt it.

"There's not enough torture in the world for this man," I say to Knox. There really isn't. Each nail feels like a tiny scrape off my need for vengeance. It's like I'm peeling a carrot, and the thinnest skin comes off with each swipe of the blade.

"Why?" the man asks Knox. "We took you in and—"

"I didn't want to be taken in. I was fine where I was. Like her father, I was just in the wrong place at the wrong time." He nods toward me.

"You're a dead man, Knox," the man says. "You know that, right?"

"I'm aware," he says. "But so are you."

"She's not one of us," the man mumbles.

"And I'm no longer one of you," Knox says.

My eyes flame with heat. They're both part of the same dark entity. It was easy to forget that sometimes, and the reminders are always painful. Especially since I'm falling for Knox.

I scream as I hammer a row of four nails up each one of Mark's outstretched arms. He screams until his voice is hoarse, but I keep going. I hammer one through his pants, right into his groin. His voice drifts, and his screams fade into a pained silence.

Knox gasps behind me. If anyone can grasp what sort of pain this asshole is experiencing, it's him.

Finally, I hammer a nail through his forehead, just like he did to my father. His pleading whispers turn to gibberish as his eyes loll in his head. His appearance haunts me. It's so similar —awake, oddly lucid, but with metal piercing his skull. My father spoke gibberish at the end too, but he was able to get out the two words I needed to find his killer.

I turn to Knox and walk into him until his back collides with the wall and his gray eyes fall to me. My hand drops to the front of his pants, and I rub over the fabric.

"Now isn't the time, karma," he whispers.

Unfortunately, I'm not in the mental space to take no for an answer.

"You need to finish him," he says, pulling my hand away.

"My father managed to crawl home with that nail in his head. He can suffer for a while. He deserves to suffer for eternity."

"This isn't you," he says. Then he swallows and looks right into my eyes. "And it's not me."

"Maybe this *is* me, Knox. Does that change things for you?"

He grabs my hand and puts it back on the front of his pants. "Does this feel like it's changed anything?"

I smirk up at him and turn toward the man nailed to the wall. He's so out of it that he keeps trying to peel himself from his confines, causing more blood to drip onto the floor. Knox is right, though. This isn't me. Not really. It makes me no better than them if I allow him to languish instead of sending him to hell where he belongs.

I grab the knife from the dresser, and Knox follows me as I approach the half-conscious man. I tug his head up by his hair and hold the blade to his throat before pressing the metal deeper and dragging the sharp edge from ear to ear. Warm, dark blood squirts from his gaping neck, splashing me.

I turn back toward Knox. A splash of blood colors his face, and another spray marks his bare chest. A scarlet jet hit my face too, dripping in thick lines down my chest and the curves of my breasts.

Knox looks at me for a moment, and before I know what's happening, he's pulled me into his chest. The blood slicks our skin as he kisses me, spreading blood anywhere we press against each other. A weight rises away from my shoulders, and I feel light. High, almost. I didn't realize just how heavy the need for vengeance had weighed on me.

Knox drags me to the bed and pushes my chest onto the mattress, then raises my skirt and cups my ass with bloody hands. He spreads my lips as he works down his slacks before pushing his warm cock inside me.

I can't help but stare at the man I killed. Weird, sadistic thoughts of Knox fucking the slit in his neck make me moan harder. I let every ill thought I've ever had join the party in my mind. Killing Sam with the blade of my knife in his ass. Gutting him as I take from him the way he's taken from me. Using his pleas like he's used mine.

"You've made me a monster," I pant, reaching to touch his thigh and grip his leg.

He leans over me, grinding his dick into me as my ass nestles into his pelvis. "You aren't a monster. You're just karma. Their actions decided yours. You only wish to give what they deserve."

"And you? What do you deserve?"

It's a question that's been pressing on my mind more and more with each passing second. How does this play out? How *can* it play out?

He pulls out of me and flips me onto my back, then puts his cock to my entrance before he pushes inside me. "You. You are all I want until my last breath. I don't know what I did to deserve you, but you're mine. Your pussy is mine. Everything I've ever done, in this or past lives, brought me right to this moment when I'm balls deep inside my own karma. The kind

I hoped for when I almost died. I don't want to be part of them anymore. I want to be part of you."

"I don't want to be beneath you," I say.

Of course I don't. I've been beneath someone for too long.

He rolls onto his back, and I climb on top of him. It's a physical representation of what he's willing to give me. He's telling me that I can be on top. I can take control when I need to.

I ride him, controlling the pace and the depth, rocking my hips on his as I chase my orgasm. He raises his hips to meet mine, rocking me forward and off balance.

I put my hand on his chest. "Stop. Let me do it myself."

By the look on his face, I'm certain he's never had a woman on top of him who held her own pleasure so high on her priority list. Now that I've gotten my vengeance, my sole focus is coming on his dick. I hope he understands, because I don't intend to stop until my body is drained from pleasure. Until every muscle aches and reminds me just how alive I am now that the man who killed my father is dead.

I lean into my hand on his chest, drop my head back, and ride Knox like it's my job. My clit rubs against his pelvis, and the piercings graze it as I lift and lower myself on him.

"Fuck me like you hate them, karma," he says through teeth-gritting pleasure.

"You ruined my life, asshole!" I scream, spreading my chest and yelling into the air. "You broke me!"

"Tell him, Allister. Tell them all!"

"And you." My glassy gaze shifts to the dead body. "You altered every fucking path in my life. You led me to Sam! You've haunted my every waking moment!"

I come down hard on his lap, getting rough enough to change his expression from pleasure to pain.

"And you." I look down at Knox. "You are the only thing I don't hate. You're the only one who hasn't hurt me, even when I deserved it." I moan as an orgasm rushes toward me, despite all my anger and frustration.

"I like you too, karma," he says, gripping my hips as he feels me getting closer. "Now come for me."

I drop forward, and his mouth devours mine. My chest rises and falls against his. Karma should absolutely be covered in blood like this. Not her own. Just the blood of the men who hurt her. The vermillion streaks meld into my skin and give me life, and I breathe that into him.

My mind is made up. I won't kill Knox. I don't know how we'll make this work, but we have to try. Instead of killing for my father, it's time to start living for him instead. He'd want me to be happy, and my greatest chance of happiness lies beneath me. It won't be easy, but nothing good in life ever is.

EPILOGUE

KNOX

Petey jumps onto my lap, and I stroke his big ears. I've never loved anything the way I love this rabbit. Hands lift him off my lap, and his big back legs kick in defiance. Soft skin replaces his warmth as Allister drapes her calves over my thighs. She sets Petey on her lap. He settles into her, spreading out with a contented sigh.

I kiss Allister. She's the only other thing that I love and the only thing that bumped ahead of Petey. She whips open the curtain behind me, letting in the country light.

We had to leave the small city of Vail. We couldn't stay in Colorado. I sealed my fate when I killed an elder, then brought another to her on a silver fucking platter. It wasn't safe for either of us.

Now we live in Wyoming in the middle of fucking nowhere. We rent a cozy country cabin, nameless, for a month at a time. I was happy to leave everything behind because everything that mattered was with me. Petey. Allister. I thought it would be harder for her, but she was packed before I even decided where we would go.

We still jump every time someone knocks on the door. We still look over our shoulders whenever we're out in public. But we look a little less each day. That's a plus.

Allister puts Petey on the ground and straddles my lap. My hand brushes her cheek—her soft, smooth, colorless skin. I make sure the girl is no longer tainted by bruises. I am many horrible things, but I won't lay my hands on Allister. Not like that.

My hand drops from her cheek to her throat. She gasps as I squeeze. Every so often, she hands the power to me and lets me put her on her back on the couch, just like this. I crawl over her, and she raises her chin.

Looking up at me, her eyes darken. "Be a good boy and let me get on your lap," she says, a playful flirt flashing on her face.

If you asked me before her if I'd ever let anyone call me a "good boy," I'd tell you to eat shit. How degrading. How emasculating.

But how fucking sexy when those words drop from her lips.

She's the only woman I've let stomp on my balls. The only one I let cut my dick and ride it until she came. The only person I'd throw my life away for. My love for her has only grown since we moved away from Vail.

She's come into her own here. Given the space and freedom she needed to thrive, she has developed a sense of herself. The weight of her father's death has lifted away. The oppressive nitpicking of an abusive boyfriend has been brushed aside. She's allowed to be whoever she wants. She's free to love whoever she wants.

And she chose me.

I've made my own changes, though I struggled more than she did. We were both held captive by abusers, but at least she wasn't trained to kill. It's been difficult to remember who I was before the Exodus dug their claws into me, and I'm not entirely there yet. But I have her, and that's all I need. She pushes me to do better every day.

I smirk down at her as I sit beside her and guide her onto my lap. I shift her shorts to the side and put my cock against her warm, wet slit.

"I'm not being a very good boy right now," I say. "Not with these dirty thoughts going through my head."

A devious smirk tugs at her lips, and instead of fucking me, she slips down my lap and onto the floor. She looks up at me, her fingers swirling around my cock.

"Maybe I'll be a good girl this one time."

For other spooky-season reads, check out these two novellas:
Last Mistake (light gray)
Books2read.com/lastmistake
Don't Stop (pitch black)
Books2read.com/Dont-Stop

Interested in Lauren's dark hitchhiker standalones? Start with
Hitched!
Books2read.com/Hitched

CONNECT WITH LAUREN

Don't miss a thing from Lauren Biel! Check out all of her books, social media connections, and other important information at Campsite.bio/LaurenBielAuthor and Lauren Biel.com

ACKNOWLEDGMENTS

To my VIP gals (Kimberly, Jessie, Nikita, Lexi, Grace), I love you so much!

The FMC shares a name (and a fierceness) with the incredible @allistersreads. Our dark-romance community is lucky to have you.

Thank you to my husband for being MY "good boy."

Brooke, my editor, you're a queen, and I appreciate you.

Thank you to my valued Patrons. Your contribution helped make this book happen.

K, Courtney, Shari, Bamsy, Electrobean, Dominique, Cris, Tia E, Tori G, Lymarie95, PaigeeBear, Sarah S, Rachel D, Kat, Helenah J, Amanda T, Tiffany M, Kala R, ______ britneyxO, Tamara M, Suzy A, Tara H, Andie J, Lisa W, Jennifer D, Court's Bookshelf, Stacy, Emily S, Sheena E, Queen Ilmaree, Serena, Susie, Virginia Saucier, Courtney Y, Gini R, Shannan T, Heather C, Kayla F, Jesi D, Charmaine B, Michelle, Karla, Christy, Melissa, Cheyanna L, Mickayla F, Kelsey S, Dani C, Sandie, SweetnSourKandy, Kayla T, Arnica S, Karly W, Cassi K, Gumdrop, Maxine T, Kay, Hamda A, Nicholetta88, Victoria S, Lori R, Jessie, Michelle M, Tabitha F, Lindsey S, Erika M, Laura T, Nicole M, Nineette W, Kimberly B, Bone-DaddyAshe, Kimberly S, Sammi Rae, Sarah, Allison B,

Andrea J, Chelle, Gabby S, Jennifer H, Jessica G, Samantha R, Sara S, Iesha E, Margaret N, April C, Amber H, Caitlyn W, Nikki, Kat De Ann, Inkeddarkreads, Jasmine, Heather S, Lizzie Borden, CryBaby, Just Jen Here, Mikasa_Kuchiki, Jada W, Briyanna M, Midwest.Kindleworm, Berthie L, Amanda C, Bailey A, YourMomReads, Laura, Eugenia M, bethbetween-thepages, Sharee S, Samantha W, Lourdes G, Kelli T, Shelby F, Lauren P, Mackenzie H, Tiannah B, Wombles, Kristiana B, Vero A, Deani, Amanda C, Brooke O, Liza M, Ashley P, Mandy G, Maddy, Courtney P, Kate, Lisa A, Leslie W, Mrs Mandy, Jordyn J, DJ Krimmer, Kayla M, Marisa, Jess M, Amber, Tiffany T, Smitty, Anna S, Barrie, Ruth, Alexandria R, Brianne, Leeat, DirtyPanda, Callie K, Christine Powell, Erica W, Ashley T

ALSO BY LAUREN BIEL

To view Lauren Biel's complete list of books, visit: https://laurenbiel.com/laurenbielbooks/

ABOUT THE AUTHOR

Lauren Biel is the author of many dark romance books, with several more titles in the works. When she's not working, she's writing. When she's not writing, she's spending time with her husband, her friends, or her pets. You might also find her on a horseback trail ride or sitting beside a waterfall in Upstate New York. When reading her work, expect the unexpected. To be the first to know about her upcoming titles, please visit www.LaurenBiel.com.